HEART OF A DOG

MIKHAIL BULGAKOV (1891-1940) was born in Kiev. After studying and practicing medicine, he gave up his career for writing. Short story writer, playwright, and novelist, Bulgakov was among the group of writers who did not emigrate after the revolution. He was under constant criticism by party-line critics, and by 1930 was completely barred from publication. It was not until recently that he has been "rehabilitated" and published again in Russia.

MIRRA GINSBURG was born in Russia. She edited and translated an anthology of satirical stories, *The Fatal Eggs and Other Soviet Satire,* in which the title story is by Bulgakov, and translated his great novel, *The Master and Margarita.* Miss Ginsburg has also translated many stories by Zamyatin, Isaac Babel, Isaac Bashevis Singer, Ilf and Petrov, Zoshchenko, and others.

Other Works by Mikhail Bulgakov
Published by Grove Press

Flight: A Play in Eight Dreams and Four Acts

The Master and Margarita

HEART OF A DOG

by

Mikhail Bulgakov

Translated by Mirra Ginsburg

GROVE PRESS, INC., New York

*Whoo-oo-oo-oo-hooh-hoo-oo! Oh, look at me, I am per-
ishing in this gateway. The blizzard roars a prayer for
the dying, and I howl with it. I am finished, finished.
That bastard in the dirty cap—the cook of the Normal
Diet Cafeteria for employees of the People's Central
Economic Soviet—threw boiling water at me and
scalded my left side. The scum, and he calls himself a
proletarian! Lord, oh lord, how it hurts! My side is
cooked to the bone. And now I howl and howl, but
what's the good of howling?*

*What harm did I do him? Would the People's Eco-
nomic Soviet get any poorer if I rooted in the garbage
heap? The greedy brute! Take a look at that mug of
his sometimes—it's wider than it's long. A crook with
a brass jowl. Ah, people, people! It was at noontime
that Dirty Cap gave me a taste of boiling water, and
now it's getting dark, it must be about four in the
afternoon, judging from the smell of onions from the
Prechistenka firehouse. The firemen get kasha for supper, as you know. But kasha is the last thing I'd eat,
like mushrooms. However, some mutts of my acquaint-
ance, from the Prechistenka, have told me that at the
Bar-Restaurant on Neglinny people gobble a fancy dish
—mushrooms en sauce piquant—at three rubles and*

1

seventy-five kopeks a portion. To each his own—to me it is like licking galoshes! Ooh-oo-oo-oo-oo . . .

My side hurts dreadfully, and I can see my future quite clearly: tomorrow I'll have sores, and, I ask you, what am I going to cure them with? In summertime, you can run down to Sokolniki Park. There is a special kind of grass there, excellent grass. Besides, you can gorge yourself on free sausage ends. And there's the greasy paper left all over by the citizens—lick it to your heart's content! And if it weren't for that nuisance who sings "Celeste Aida" in the field under the moon so that your heart sinks, it would be altogether perfect. But where can you go now? Were you kicked with a boot? You were. Were you hit with a brick in the ribs? Time and again. I've tasted everything, but I've made peace with my fate, and if I'm whining now, it's only because of the pain and the cold—because my spirit hasn't yet gone out of my body. . . . A dog is hard to kill, his spirit clings to life.

But my body is broken and battered, it's taken its share of punishment from people. And the worst of it is that the boiling water he slopped over me ate right through the fur, and now my left side is without protection of any kind. I can very easily contract pneumonia, and once I do, my dear citizens, I'll die of hunger. With pneumonia, you're supposed to lie under the stairs in a front hallway. But who will run around for me, a sick bachelor dog, and look for sustenance in garbage heaps? Once my lung is affected, I'll be crawling on my belly, feeble as a pup, and anyone can knock the daylight out of me with a stick. And then the janitors with their badges will grab me by the feet and throw me on the garbage collector's cart.

Of all the proletarians, janitors are the worst trash. Human dregs—the lowest category. Cooks can be of all sorts. For example, the late Vlas from Prechistenka.

How many lives he saved! Because the main thing is to get a bite to eat when you're sick. All the old dogs still talk of how Vlas would throw them a bone, and with a solid chunk of meat on it. May he be blessed for it in the Heavenly Kingdom—a real personality he was, the gentry's cook for the Counts Tolstoy, not one of those nobodies from the Soviet of Normal Diet. The things they do in that Normal Diet, it's more than a dog's brain can comprehend. Those scoundrels make soup of stinking corned beef, and the poor wretches don't know what they're eating. They come running, gobbling it down, lapping it up.

Take that little typist, ninth grade, getting four and a half chervontsy. True enough, her lover will give her a pair of Persian cotton stockings once in a while. But what won't she have to put up with for that Persian cotton? You may be sure he will not take her in some ordinary way, no, he'll insist on French love. They're scum, those Frenchmen, between you and me. Although they know how to eat, and everything with red wine. Yes . . . So she'll come running, this little typist. On four and a half chervontsy, after all, you can't afford to eat at the Bar-Restaurant. She doesn't even have enough for a movie, and a movie is the only solace in a woman's life. She shudders and makes faces, but she puts away the stinking soup. . . . Just to think of it: a two-course meal for forty kopeks; and both courses together aren't worth fifteen kopeks, because the manager has pocketed the other twenty-five. And is that the kind of nourishment she needs? The tip of her right lung isn't quite right, and she has female trouble from that French love of his, and they've deducted from her wages at work, and fed her putrid meat at the cafeteria. But there she is, there she is . . . running toward the gateway in her lover's stockings. Her feet are cold, her stomach's cold because her fur's

*like mine now, and her panties give no warmth, a bit
of lacy fluff. For her lover's sake. Let her just try and
put on flannel panties, and he'll yell: but how inelegant
you are! I'm fed up with my Matrena, I've had enough
of flannel pants, it's my turn to have some fun in life.
I'm chairman now, and whatever I filch, all of it goes
for female flesh, for lobster tails, for Abrau-D'urso
wine. Because I've been starved long enough in my
youth, I've had it, and there's no life after death.*

*I am sorry for her, so sorry! But I'm even sorrier
for myself. I'm not saying this out of selfishness, but
because our conditions really don't compare. At least,
she is warm at home, and I, I . . . Where can I go?
Oo-oo-oo-ooh!*

"Tsk, tsk, tsk! Sharik, hey, Sharik . . . Why are you
whimpering, poor beast? Who hurt you? Ah-h!"

The wind, that raging witch, rattled the gate and
boxed the young lady on the ear with its broom. It blew
up her skirt above her knees, baring the cream-colored
stockings and a narrow strip of the poorly laundered
lace panties. It drowned out her words and swept across
the dog.

"Good God . . . What weather . . . Oh . . . And my
stomach hurts. It's that corned beef, that corned beef!
When will it all end?"

Ducking her head, the young lady threw herself into
attack, broke through the gates, and out into the street;
the blizzard began to spin and spin her around, push
her this way and that, till she became a column of
swirling snow and disappeared.

And the dog remained in the gateway. Suffering
from his mutilated side, he pressed himself to the cold
wall, gasped for air, and firmly decided that he would
not go anywhere from there, he'd die right there in the

HEART OF A DOG

gateway. Despair overwhelmed him. He felt so bitter and sore at heart, so lonely and terrified, that tiny dog's tears like little bubbles exuded from his eyes and dried at once. Frozen tufts of fur hung from his mangled side, and among them the bare scalded spots showed ominously red. How senseless, stupid, and cruel cooks are. "Sharik" she called him. . . . "Little Ball" . . . What kind of a "Sharik" is he, anyway? Sharik is somebody round, plump, silly, a son of aristocratic parents who gobbles oatmeal, and he is shaggy, lanky, tattered, skinny as a rail, a homeless mutt. But thanks for a kind word, anyway.

The door of the brightly lit store across the street swung open and a citizen came out of it. Yes, precisely, a citizen, not a comrade. Or even, to be more exact, a gentleman. The closer he came, the clearer it was.

A gentleman. Do you think I judge by the coat? Nonsense. Many proletarians are also wearing coats nowadays. True, their collars aren't quite like this one, naturally. But from a distance it is easy to confuse them. No, it is the eyes I'm talking about. When you look at the eyes, you can't mistake a man, from near or far. Oh, the eyes are an important thing. Like a barometer. You can see everything in them—the man whose soul is dry as dust, the man who'll never kick you in the ribs with the tip of his boot, and the man who is afraid of everything himself. It's the last kind, the lickspittle, whom it is sometimes a pleasure to grab by the ankle. Afraid? Get it, then. If you're afraid, you must deserve it. . . . Rr-r-r . . . Rr-r-r! . . .

The gentleman confidently crossed the street wrapped in a column of swirling snow and stepped into the gateway. *Oh, yes, you can tell everything about him. This one won't gobble moldy corned beef, and if anybody*

*serves it to him, he'll raise hell, he'll write to the news-
papers: "I, Philip Philippovich, was fed such and
such."*

*He is coming closer and closer. This one eats well
and does not steal. He won't kick you, but he isn't
afraid of anything himself. And he is not afraid because he is never hungry. He is a gentleman engaged
in mental work, with a sculptured, pointed goatee and
a gray, fluffy, dashing mustache, like those worn by
the old French knights. But the smell he spreads
through the snow is rotten, a hospital smell. And
cigars.*

*What devil, do you think, could have brought him to
the Central Economic Administration cooperative?
There he is, right by me . . . What is he waiting for?
Oo-oo-oo-oo . . . What could he have bought in that
shabby little store, isn't Okhotny Ryad enough for
him? What's that? Sausage! Sir, if you could see what
this sausage is made of, you'd never come near that
store. Better give it to me.*

The dog gathered his last remnant of strength and
crawled in a frenzy from under the gateway to the sidewalk. The blizzard clattered over his head like gun-
shots, and swept up the huge letters on a canvas plac-
ard, IS REJUVENATION POSSIBLE?

*Naturally, it's possible. The smell rejuvenated me,
lifted me from my belly, contracted my stomach, empty
for the last two days, with fiery spasms. The smell that
conquered the hospital smells, the heavenly smell of
chopped horsemeat with garlic and pepper. I sense, I
know—the sausage is in the right-hand pocket of his
overcoat. He stands over me. Oh, my lord and master!
Glance at me. I am dying. We have the souls of slaves,
and a wretched fate!*

The dog crawled on his belly like a snake, weeping

bitter tears. *Observe the cook's work. But you'll never give me anything. Oh, I know the rich very well! But actually, what do you need it for? What do you want with putrid horsemeat? You'll never get such poison as they sell you at the Moscow Agricultural Industries stores anywhere else. And you have had your lunch today, you, a personage of world importance, thanks to male sex glands. Oo-oo-oo-oo . . . What's happening in this world? But it seems too early to die, and despair is truly a sin. I must lick his hands, there's nothing else left.*

The mysterious gentleman bent over the dog, the gold rims of his glasses flashed, and he took a long, white package from his right pocket. Without removing his brown gloves, he unwrapped the paper, which was immediately snatched up by the blizzard, and broke off a piece of what is known as "special Cracow sausage." And he held it out to the dog. *Oh, generous soul! Oo-oo-oo!*

"Whuit-whuit," the gentleman whistled and added in the sternest tone: "Take it! Sharik, Sharik!"

Sharik again. They'd christened me. But call me what you will. For such an exceptional deed!

The dog instantly pulled off the skin, sank his teeth with a sob into the Cracow sausage, and gobbled it up in a wink. And almost choked to tears on the sausage and the snow, because in his greed he had almost swallowed the cord. *I'll lick your hand now, again, again. I kiss your trousers, my benefactor!*

"Enough for now . . ." The gentleman spoke curtly, as though issuing commands. He bent down to Sharik, peered into his eyes, and suddenly passed his gloved hand intimately and caressingly over Sharik's belly.

"Ah," he said significantly. "No collar. That's fine, you're just what I need. Come on, follow me." He snapped his fingers, "Whuit, whuit!"

Follow you? Why, to the end of the world. You may kick me with your fine suede shoes, I wouldn't say a word.

The street lights gleamed all along the Prechistenka. His side ached intolerably, but Sharik forgot the pain from time to time, possessed by a single thought: he must not lose the wonderful vision in the overcoat in the crowd, he must do something to express his love and devotion. And he expressed it seven times along the stretch of Prechistenka up to Obukhov Lane. At Dead Man's Alley he kissed the man's overshoe. He cleared the way for him. Once he frightened a lady so badly with his wild howl that she plopped down on a fire pump. Twice he whimpered, to keep alive the man's sympathy for him.

A mangy stray tom, pretending to be Siberian, dived out from behind a drainpipe; he had caught a whiff of the sausage despite the storm. Sharik went blind with rage at the thought that the rich eccentric who picked up wounded mutts in gateways might take it into his head to bring along that thief as well, and then he'd be obliged to share the product of the Moscow Agricultural Industries with him. He snapped his teeth at the tom so furiously that the tom shot up the drainpipe to the second story, hissing like a torn hose. Gr-r-r-r . . . Wow! Feed every ragged tramp hanging around the Prechistenka!

The gentleman appreciated his devotion: as they reached the firehouse, he stopped by the window from which the pleasant rumbling of a French horn could be heard and rewarded him with a second piece, a bit smaller, just a couple of ounces.

Ah, the silly man. He's trying to tempt me on. Don't worry, I won't run off. I'll follow you anywhere you say.

"Whuit-whuit-whuit! Here!"

Obukhov Lane? Certainly. I know the lane very well.

"Whuit-whuit!"

Here? With plea . . . Oh, no, if you don't mind. No. There's a doorman here. And there's nothing worse in the world. Much more dangerous than janitors. A thoroughly hateful breed. Even viler than toms. Murderers in gold braid.

"Don't be afraid, come."

"How do you do, Philip Philippovich?"

"Hello, Fyodor."

That's a man for you! Heavens, to whom has my dog's fate brought me? What sort of personage is this who can bring dogs from the street past doormen into the house? Look at that scoundrel—not a sound, not a move! True, his eyes are chilly, but on the whole he is indifferent under that gold-braided cap. As if everything's just as it should be. He respects the gentleman, and how he respects him! Well, and I am with him, and walk in after him. Didn't dare to touch me, did you? Put that in your craw. Wouldn't I love to sink my teeth into your calloused proletarian foot! For all we've suffered from your king. How many times did you bloody my nose with a broom, eh?

"Come on, come on."

I understand, I understand, don't worry. Wherever you go, I'll follow. Just show the way, I won't fall back, despite my miserable side.

From the staircase, calling down: "Were there no letters for me, Fyodor?"

From below, up the stairs, deferentially: "No, Sir, Philip Philippovich." Then confidentially, intimately, in a lowered voice, "They've moved in some more tenants, settled them in Number Three."

The lordly benefactor of dogs turned sharply on the step, bent over the rail and asked in a horrified voice:

"Real-ly?"

His eyes became round and his mustache bristled.

The doorman turned up his face, put his cupped hand to his lips, and confirmed it:

"Yes, sir, four of them."

"Good God! I can imagine what bedlam they'll have in the apartment now. And what do they say?"

"Why, nothing."

"And Fyodor Pavlovich?"

"He went to get some screens and brick. They'll build partitions."

"Damned outrage!"

"They'll be moving additional tenants into all the apartments, Philip Philippovich, except yours. There's just been a meeting, they elected a new committee and kicked the old one out."

"The things that are going on. Ai-ai-ai . . . Whuit, whujt."

I'm coming, I'm keeping up. My side is bothering me, you know. Allow me to lick your boot.

The doorman's braid disappeared below. The radiators on the marble landing exuded warmth. Another turn, and we're on the second floor.

II

There is absolutely no necessity to learn how to read; meat smells a mile off, anyway. Nevertheless, if you live in Moscow and have a brain in your head, you'll pick up reading willy-nilly, and without attending any courses. Out of the forty thousand or so Moscow dogs, only a total idiot won't know how to read the word "sausage."

Sharik first began to learn by color. When he was only four months old, blue-green signs with the letters MSPO—indicating a meat store—appeared all over Moscow. I repeat, there was no need for any of them— you can smell meat anyway. But one day Sharik made a mistake. Tempted by an acid-blue sign, Sharik, whose sense of smell had been knocked out by the exhaust of a passing car, dashed into an electric supplies store instead of a butcher shop. The store was on Myasnitsky Street and was owned by the Polubizner Bros. The brothers gave the dog a taste of insulated wire, and that is even neater than a cabby's whip. That famous moment may be regarded as the starting point of Sharik's education. Back on the sidewalk, he began to realize that blue didn't always mean "meat." Howling with the fiery pain, his tail pressed down between his legs, he recalled that over all the butcher shops there

11

was a red or golden wiggle—the first one on the left—that looked like a sled.

After that, his learning proceeded by leaps and bounds. He learned the letter "t" from "Fish Trust" on the corner of Mokhovaya, and then the letter "s" (it was handier for him to approach the store from the tail end of the word, because of the militiaman who stood near the beginning of the "Fish").

Tile squares set into corner houses in Moscow always and inevitably meant "cheese." A black samovar faucet over the word indicated the former owner of Chichkin's, piles of red Holland cheese, beastly salesmen who hated dogs, sawdust on the floor, and that most disgusting, evil-smelling Beckstein.

If somebody was playing an accordion, which was not much better than "Celeste Aida," and there was a smell of frankfurters, the first letters on the white signs very conveniently added up to the words "no inde . . . ," which meant "no indecent language and no tips." In such places there were occasional messy brawls and people got hit in the face with fists, and sometimes with napkins or boots.

If there were stale hams hanging in a window and tangerines on the sill, it meant . . . Grr . . . grr . . . groceries. And if there were dark bottles with a vile liquid, it meant . . . Wwhi-w-i-wines . . . The former Yeliseyev Brothers.

The unknown gentleman who had brought the dog to the doors of his luxurious apartment on the second floor rang, and the dog immediately raised his eyes to the large black card with gold letters next to the wide door with panes of wavy pink glass. He put together the first three letters right away: Pe-ar-o, "Pro." After that came a queer little hooked stick, nasty looking, unfamiliar. No telling what it meant. Could it be "proletarian"? Sharik wondered with astonishment

. . . No, impossible. He raised his nose, sniffed the coat again, and said to himself with certainty: Oh, no, there's nothing proletarian in this smell. Some fancy, learned word, who knows what it means.

A sudden, joyous light flared up behind the pink glass, setting off the black card still more clearly. The door swung open silently, and a pretty young woman in a white apron and a lace cap appeared before the dog and his master. The former felt a gust of divine warmth, and the fragrance of lilies of the valley came at him from the woman's skirt.

That's something, that's really something, thought the dog.

"Come in, please, Mr. Sharik," the gentleman invited him ironically, and Sharik stepped in reverently, wagging his tail.

A multitude of objects crowded the rich foyer. He was most impressed with the mirror from floor to ceiling, which immediately reflected a second bedraggled, lacerated Sharik, the terrifying stag's horns up above, the numerous overcoats and boots, and the opalescent tulip with an electric light under the ceiling.

"Where did you dig him up, Philip Philippovich?" the woman asked, smiling and helping the gentleman to remove his heavy overcoat lined with silver fox, shimmering with bluish glints. "Heavens! What a mangy cur!"

"Nonsense. Where is he mangy?" the gentleman rapped out sternly.

Having removed the coat, he was now seen wearing a black suit of English cloth, with a gold chain gleaming discreetly and pleasantly across his stomach.

"Wait, stop wriggling, whuit . . . stop wriggling, you silly. Hm! . . . This isn't mange . . . wait a minute, you devil . . . Hm! A-ah. It's a burn. What scoundrel did it to you? Eh? Be still a moment, will you! . . ."

A cook, a bastard of a cook! The dog said with his piteous eyes and whimpered a little.

"Zina," commanded the gentleman, "take him to the examination room at once, and get me a smock."

The woman whistled, snapped her fingers, and the dog, after a moment's hesitation, followed her. They came into a narrow, dimly lit hallway, passed one laquered door, walked to the end, turned left, and found themselves in a dark little room which the dog immediately disliked for its ominous smell. The darkness clicked and turned into blinding daylight, and he was dazzled by the glitter, shine, and whiteness all around.

Oh, no, the dog howled mentally. Excuse me, but I won't, I won't let you! Now I understand it, to hell with them and their sausage. They've tricked me into a dog hospital. Now they'll make me lap castor oil, and cut up my whole side with knives, and I cannot bear to have it touched as it is.

"Hey, stop, where are you going?" cried the woman called Zina.

The dog spun around, coiled himself like a spring, and suddenly threw himself at the door with his sound side so that the crash was heard all through the apartment. Then he sprang back and whirled on the spot like a top, turning over a white pail and sending the tufts of cotton it contained flying in all directions. As he spun, the walls lined with cases full of glittering instruments danced around him; the white apron and the screaming, distorted female face bobbed up and down.

"Where do you think you're going, you shaggy devil?" Zina cried desperately. "Damned cur!"

Where is their back staircase? wondered the dog. He dashed himself at random at a glass door, hoping it was a second exit. A shower of splinters scattered, ringing and clattering, then a potbellied jar flew out, and the reddish muck in it instantly spread over the floor, raising a stench. The real door flew open.

"Wait, you brute," shouted the gentleman, jumping around, with one arm in the sleeve of the smock, trying to catch the dog by the leg. "Zina, grab him by the scruff, the bastard!"

"My . . . oh, my, what a dog!"

The door opened still wider and another male individual in a smock burst in. Crushing the broken glass, he rushed, not to the dog, but to an instrument case, opened it, and the whole room filled with a sweetish, nauseating smell. Then the individual threw himself upon the dog, pressing him down with his belly; in the course of the struggle the dog managed to snap enthusiastically at his leg just above the shoe. The individual gasped, but did not lose control. The nauseous liquid stopped the dog's breath and his head began to reel. Then his legs dropped off, and he slid off somewhere sideways. Thank you, it's all over, he thought dreamily, dropping right on the sharp splinters. Goodbye Moscow! Never again will I see Chichkin's and proletarians and Cracow sausage. I'm off to paradise for my long patience in this dog's life. Brothers, murderers, why are you doing it to me?

And he rolled over on his side and gave up the ghost.

When he revived, his head was turning vaguely and he had a queasy feeling at the pit of his stomach. As for his side, it did not exist, his side was blissfully silent. The dog opened his languorous right eye and saw out of the corner of it that he was tightly bandaged across the sides and stomach. So they've had their will of me, the sons of bitches, after all, he thought mistily. It was a neat job, though, in all justice.

"From Seville and to Granada . . . on a quiet, dusky night," a voice sang over him absently, off key.

The dog, surprised, opened both his eyes wide and

beheld a man's leg on a white stool two steps away from him. The trousers and underpants were turned up, and the bare yellow calf was smeared with dried blood and iodine.

Saints in heaven! thought the dog. I must have bitten him. It's my work. I'm in for a whipping now!

"There are sounds of serenading, and a clashing of bared swords! Why did you bite the doctor, you tramp? Eh? Why did you break the glass? Eh?"

Oo-oo-oo . . . the dog whimpered pathetically.

"All right, all right. You've come to? Just lie there quietly, dumbbell."

"How did you manage to get such a nervous dog to follow you?" asked a pleasant masculine voice, and the trouser leg was rolled down. There was a smell of tobacco, and the glass jars tinkled in one of the cases.

"By kindness. The only method possible in dealing with living creatures. By terror you cannot get anywhere with an animal, no matter what its stage of development. I've always asserted this, I assert it today, and I shall go on asserting it. They are wrong thinking that terror will help them. No—no, it won't, whatever its color: white, red, or even brown! Terror completely paralyzes the nervous system. Zina! I bought this scoundrel some Cracow sausage, a ruble and forty kopeks' worth. Be good enough to feed him as soon as he stops feeling nauseous."

The glass splinters crackled as they were swept out and a woman's voice remarked coquettishly:

"Cracow sausage! Heavens, twenty kopeks' worth of scraps from the butcher shop would have been good enough for him. I'd rather eat the Cracow sausage myself."

"Just try! I'll show you how to eat it! It's poison for the human stomach. A grown-up girl, and she's ready to stuff herself with every kind of garbage, like a baby.

Don't you dare! I warn you: neither I, nor Dr. Bormenthal will bother with you when you come down with stomach cramps. . . . And if anyone says you can be easily replaced . . ."

A soft, delicate tinkling scattered through the apartment, and voices were heard from the distant foyer. The telephone rang. Zina disappeared.

Philip Philippovich threw his cigarette butt into the pail, buttoned his smock, smoothed down the fluffy mustache before the small mirror on the wall, and called the dog:

"Whuit, whuit. All right, all right. Come on, we'll see our patients."

The dog rose unsteadily, swayed and trembled, but quickly recovered and followed the flying coattails of Philip Philippovich. Once more the dog crossed the narrow hallway, but now it was lit by a bright rosette on the ceiling. And when the laquered door opened, he entered the office with Philip Philippovich and was dazzled by its interior. To begin with, it blazed with lights: lights burning under the molded ceiling, on the table, on the walls, lights flashing from the glass doors of the cabinets. The lights illuminated a multitude of objects, the most intriguing of which was the huge owl perched on a twig projecting from the wall.

"Lie down," ordered Philip Philippovich.

The carved door across the room opened, and the man Sharik had nipped on the leg came in. In the bright light he turned out to be young and extremely handsome, with a small, pointed beard. He handed Philip Philippovich a sheet of paper and said:

"The same one . . ."

He disappeared, and Philip Philippovich spread the tails of his smock, sat down at a huge desk, and immediately became extraordinarily dignified and important.

No, this is not a clinic, it's something else, the dog

thought in confusion, stretching himself on the patterned rug near the heavy leather sofa. As for that owl, we'll have to find out about it. . . .

The door opened softly, and the man who entered was so disconcerting to the dog, that he gave a short, timid bark.

"Quiet! Well, well, but you're unrecognizable, my friend."

The visitor bowed with great respect and some embarrassment.

"He-he! You are a wizard, a miracle worker, Professor," he mumbled with confusion.

"Take off your trousers, my friend," commanded Philip Philippovich, getting up.

Jesus Christ, thought the dog, what a queer bird!

The hair on the visitor's head was completely green, and at the nape it had a rusty, tobacco-brown tinge. His face was covered with wrinkles, but its color was baby-pink. His left knee did not bend, and he had to drag his leg over the carpet, but his right foot jumped like a jumping jack's. In the lapel of his magnificent coat a precious stone gleamed like an eye.

The dog was so excited and curious that he forgot his nausea.

Tiaw, tiaw! . . . he yipped tentatively.

"Quiet! How do you sleep, my dear?"

"He-he. Are we alone, Professor? It's indescribable," the visitor spoke with embarrassment. "Parole d'honneur, I remember nothing like it for twenty-five years," the queer individual pulled at his trouser button. "Will you believe me, Professor, every night it's flocks of naked girls. I am positively enchanted. You are a magician."

"Hm," Philip Philippovich grunted thoughtfully, peering into the guest's pupils.

The latter had finally mastered his buttons and

removed the striped trousers. Under them the dog beheld a pair of the most unique underpants. They were cream colored, embroidered with black cats, and they smelled of perfume.

The cats proved too much, and the dog gave such a bark that the individual jumped.

"Ai!"

"I'll thrash you! Don't be afraid, he doesn't bite."

I don't bite? the dog thought with astonishment.

A little envelope dropped out of the visitor's trouser pocket, with a picture of a beauty with loose, flowing hair. He jumped up, bent down, picked it up and flushed darkly.

"Look out, though," Philip Philippovich warned gloomily, shaking a finger at him. "After all, don't overdo it!"

"I don't over . . . ." the visitor mumbled in confusion, continuing to undress. "It was only as a sort of experiment, my dear Professor."

"And? How did it go?" Philip Philippovich asked sternly.

The odd visitor only raised his hands in ecstasy.

"I swear, nothing like it for twenty-five years, Professor. The last time was in 1899 in Paris, on Rue de la Paix."

"And what made you turn green?"

The visitor's face clouded over.

"That damned liquid! You can't imagine, Professor, what those good-for-nothings stuck me with instead of dye. Just look at it," he muttered, searching for a mirror with his eyes. "They ought to get their teeth bashed in!" he added, suddenly furious. "What am I to do now, Professor?" he asked tearfully.

"Hm, shave it off."

"Professor," the visitor exclaimed piteously, "but it'll grow back gray again. Besides, I won't be able to show my face at the office. I haven't gone in for three days as it is. Ah, Professor, if you would only discover a method of rejuvenating the hair as well!"

"Not all at once, my friend, not all at once," mumbled Philip Philippovich.

He bent down and examined the patient's naked stomach with glittering eyes.

"Well—charming, everything is in perfect order. To tell the truth, I really didn't expect such results. New blood, new songs. Get dressed, my friend!"

"My love is the most beautiful of all! . . ." the patient sang out in a voice that quavered like a frying pan struck with a fork, and began to dress, his face beaming. Then, bobbing up and down and spreading the odor of perfume, he counted out a bundle of large bills, handed them to Philip Philippovich, and tenderly pressed both his hands.

"You need not report for two weeks," said Philip Philippovich, "but I must repeat, be careful."

"Professor!" the man's voice exclaimed ecstastically from behind the door, "you may be quite, quite sure," and he vanished with a sugary giggle.

The tinkling of the bell spread throughout the apartment, the laquered door opened, the bitten one entered and gave Philip Philippovich another sheet of paper, saying:

"The age is entered incorrectly. Must be fifty or fifty-five. The heart tone is somewhat flat."

He disappeared, to be replaced by a rustling lady in a hat set at a jaunty angle and with a gleaming necklace on her flabby, wrinkled neck. She had peculiar dark bags under her eyes, and her cheeks were as red as a doll's. She was very nervous.

"My dear lady! How old are you?" Philip Philippovich asked very sternly.

The lady became frightened and even turned pale under the coat of rouge.

"I . . . Professor, I swear, if you only knew my tragedy! . . ."

"How old are you, madam?" Philip Philippovich repeated still more sternly.

"Honestly. . . Well, forty-five. . ."

"Madam," roared Philip Philippovich, "people are waiting to see me. Don't waste my time, please. You're not the only one!"

The lady's breast heaved stormily.

"I'll tell it to you alone, as a luminary of science. But I swear, it is so dreadful."

"How old are you?" Philip Philippovich squealed in fury and his eyeglasses glinted.

"Fifty-one," the lady answered, shrinking with fear.

"Take off your pants, madam," Philip Philippovich said with relief and pointed to a high white platform in the corner.

"I swear, Professor," the lady mumbled, undoing some snaps on her belt with trembling fingers. "That Maurice . . . I tell this to you as at confessional . . . ."

"From Seville and to Granada," Philip Philippovich sang absently and pressed the pedal of the marble washstand. The water rushed out.

"I swear by God," the lady said, and spots of genuine red stood out under the artificial ones on her cheeks. "I know—this is my last passion. But he is such a scoundrel! Oh, Professor! He is a cardsharp, all of Moscow knows it. He's ready to take up with every nasty little seamstress. He is so fiendishly young!" The lady muttered, kicking off a crumpled bit of lace from under her rustling skirts.

The dog was utterly bewildered, and everything turned upside down in his head.

The devil with you, he thought dimly, putting his head down on his paws and dozing off with shame. I wouldn't even try to figure it out—I couldn't make head or tail of it anyway.

He was awakened by a clinking sound and saw that Philip Philippovich had thrown some shiny tubes into a basin.

The spotty lady, her hands pressed to her chest, was looking at Philip Philippovich with anxious hope. The latter frowned importantly, then sat down at his desk and wrote something.

"We'll do a transplant. A monkey's ovaries," he declared, looking at her sternly.

"Ah, Professor, a monkey's?"

"Yes," he replied implacably.

"And when is the operation?" she asked in a faint voice, turning pale.

"From Seville and to Granada. . . Uhm . . . on Monday. You'll come to the hospital in the morning. My assistant will prepare you."

"Ah, Professor, I'd rather not go to the hospital. Can't it be done here, Professor?"

"Well, you see, I operate here only in special cases. And it will be very expensive—fifty chervontsy."

"I am willing, Professor!"

The water clattered again, the hat with the feathers swayed, a head appeared, bare as a platter, and embraced Philip Philippovich. The dog dozed, his nausea gone. His side no longer troubled him, he luxuriated in the warmth, and even caught a quick nap and saw a fragment of a pleasant dream, in which he managed to pull a whole tuft of feathers out of the owl's tail. . . .

And then an agitated voice barked over his head:

"I am too well known in Moscow, Professor. What am I to do?"

"Gentlemen," Philip Philippovich cried indignantly, "this is impossible. A man must control himself. How old is she?"

"Fourteen, Professor . . . You understand, the publicity will ruin me. I am slated to receive an assignment abroad in a day or two."

"But I am not a lawyer, my friend . . . . Well, wait two years and marry her."

"I am married, Professor."

"Ah, gentlemen, gentlemen!"

The doors opened and closed, faces succeeded one another, the instruments in the cases clattered, and Philip Philippovich worked without a moment's respite.

What an obscene place, the dog thought, but how pleasant! And what the devil did he need me for? Will he really let me stay here? Such an eccentric! Why, he need only blink an eye and he could have the finest dog in town! But maybe I am handsome? I guess I'm lucky! But that owl is trash . . . . Insolent trash.

The dog came to completely only late in the evening, when the bell ceased ringing, and precisely at the moment when the door opened and let in a special group of visitors. There were four of them at once. All of them young men, and all very modestly dressed.

What do they want? the dog thought with astonishment. Philip Philippovich met his guests with even less cordiality. He stood near his desk and stared at them as a general would at the enemy. The nostrils of his hawklike nose flared out. The visitors shifted their feet on the rug.

"We've come to you, Professor," began the one with

a shock of thick curly hair standing up at least six inches above his face, "to talk about . . ."

"You should not go about without galoshes in such weather, gentlemen," Philip Philippovich interrupted him didactically. "To begin with, you will catch colds. Secondly, you've tracked up my rugs, and all my rugs are Persian."

The fellow with the shock of hair fell silent, and all four stared at Philip Philippovich with astonishment. The silence lasted several seconds, broken only by the tapping of Philip Philippovich's fingers on the painted wooden platter on his desk.

"To begin with," the youngest of the four, with a peachlike face, brought out finally, "we are not gentlemen."

"And secondly," Philip Philippovich interrupted him, "are you a man or a woman?"

The four lapsed into silence again, gaping with open mouths. This time the fellow with the hair recovered first.

"What is the difference, comrade?" he asked proudly.

"I am a woman," confessed the peach-faced youth in the leather jacket, blushing violently. And for some unknown reason, another visitor—with blond hair and a cossack hat—also turned a vivid red.

"In that case, you may keep your cap on. As for you, dear sir, I must ask you to remove your headgear," Philip Philippovich said weightily.

"I'm no dear sir to you," the blond man answered sharply, removing his hat.

"We have come to you," the dark one with the shock of hair began once more.

"First of all, who is 'we'?"

"We are the new house management committee," the dark one said with controlled rage. "I am Shvonder, she is Vyazemskaya, he is Comrade Pestrukhin, and this is Sharovkyan. And so, we . . ."

"Are you the people they've moved into Fyodor Pavlovich Sablin's apartment?"

"We are," confirmed Shvonder.

"Good God, the Kalabukhov house is finished!" Philip Philippovich exclaimed in despair, clapping his hands together.

"Are you joking, Professor?"

"Joking? I am in total despair," Philip Philippovich cried. "What's going to happen to the steam heat now?"

"You're mocking us, Professor Preobrazhensky?"

"What business brought you to me? Make it short, I am just going to dinner."

"We are the house management," Shvonder spoke with hatred. "We've come to you after a general meeting of the tenants of this house which went into the question of consolidating the tenancy of the apartments. . . ."

"Who went into whom?" Philip Philippovich shouted. "Be kind enough to express yourself more clearly."

"The question of consolidation."

"That will do! I understand! Are you aware of the resolution of August 12 which exempted my apartment from any of your consolidations or tenant transfers?"

"We are," answered Shvonder. "But the general meeting reviewed your case and came to the conclusion that, generally and on the whole, you occupy excessive space. Altogether excessive. You live alone in seven rooms."

"I live and work in seven rooms," replied Philip Philippovich, "and I would like to have an eighth one. I need it most urgently for a library."

The four were stunned.

"An eighth one! O-ho," said the blond man who had

been ordered to remove his headgear. "Really, that's a good one!"

"It's indescribable!" cried the youth who had turned out to be a woman.

"I have a waiting room which, please note, is also a library; a dining room; and my office. That makes three. The examination room makes four, the operating room, five. My bedroom, six, and my servant's room, seven. And I haven't enough space. . . . However, all this is beside the point. My apartment is exempt, and that's the end of it. May I go to dinner now?"

"Excuse me," said the fourth visitor, who looked like a firm, strong beetle.

"Excuse me," Shvonder interrupted him, "this is precisely what we have come to talk to you about—the dining room and the examination room. The general meeting asks you voluntarily and by way of labor discipline to give up your dining room. Nobody has a dining room in Moscow."

"Not even Isadora Duncan," the woman cried in a ringing voice.

Something happened to Philip Philippovich, as a result of which his delicate face turned purple, and he did not utter a sound, waiting to see what happened next.

"And the examination room too," continued Shvonder. "The examination room can perfectly well be combined with the office."

"Uhum," said Philip Philippovich in a strange voice. "And where am I to take my meals?"

"In the bedroom," the four answered in chorus.

The purple of Philip Philippovich's face assumed a grayish tinge.

"Eat in the bedroom," he said in a slightly choked voice, "read in the examination room, dress in the waiting room, operate in the maid's room, and examine

patients in the dining room. It is very possible that
Isadora Duncan does just this. Perhaps she dines in
her office and dissects rabbits in the bathroom. Perhaps. But I am not Isadora Duncan! . . ." he barked
out suddenly, and the purple of his face turned yellow.
"I shall dine in the dining room, and operate in the
surgery! You may report this to the general meeting,
and now I beg you to return to your respective business
and allow me to take my meal where all normal people
take theirs, that is, in the dining room, and not in the
foyer or the nursery."

"In that case, Professor, in view of your obstinate
opposition," said the excited Shvonder, "we shall lodge
a complaint against you with the higher authorities."

"Ah," said Philip Philippovich, "so?" and his voice
assumed a suspiciously polite tone. "I will ask you to
wait just a moment."

That's a man for you, the dog thought with admiration. Just like me. Oh, but he'll nip them in a second,
oh, but he'll nip them. I don't know yet how he'll do it,
but he'll do a job of it. . . . Get 'em! That leggy one,
he ought to be grabbed just above the boot, right at
that tendon behind the knee . . . ur-r-r . . .

Philip Philippovich banged the receiver as he lifted
it from the telephone and said into it:

"Please . . . yes . . . thank you. Ask Pyotr Alexandrovich to the telephone, please. Professor Preobrazhensky. Pyotr Alexandrovich? I am glad I found you in.
Thank you, quite well. Pyotr Alexandrovich, your
operation is canceled. And all the other operations as
well. This is why: I am discontinuing my work in
Moscow, and in Russia generally. . . . Four individuals
have just come in, one of them a woman dressed as a
man, and two armed with revolvers, and they're trying
to intimidate me in my home in order to take it from
me."

"But, Professor," Shvonder began, changing in the face.

"Sorry . . . I cannot repeat everything they said. I am not a fancier of nonsense. Suffice it to say that they suggested that I give up my examination room. In other words, they make it necessary for me to operate on you in the place where I usually dissect rabbits. I not only cannot, but have no right to work under such conditions. Therefore I am discontinuing my activities, closing my apartment, and leaving for Sochi. I can turn the keys over to Shvonder. Let him operate."

The four stood petrified. The snow was melting on their boots.

"What can I do? . . . I find it very unpleasant myself. . . . What? Oh, no, Pyotr Alexandrovich! Oh, no. I refuse to go on any more. I'm at the end of my patience. This is the second time since August. . . . What? Hm . . . If you wish. Very well. But on one condition: I don't care who, when, or what, but it must be an order that will make sure that neither Shvonder, nor anyone else will be allowed even to approach the door of my apartment. A final and definitive order. An absolute one! A real one! Ironclad. So that my name is never mentioned again. Finished. I'm dead to them. Yes, yes. Please. Who will? Ah . . . That's something else. Aha . . . Good. I'll give him the receiver now. Be so kind," Philip Philippovich spoke in a serpentine voice to Shvonder, "he'll speak to you now."

"But please, Professor," said Shvonder, flushing and turning pale, "you have misrepresented our words."

"I'll thank you not to use such expressions."

Shvonder, completely abashed, took the receiver and said:

"I'm listening. Yes . . . Chairman of the house committee . . . But we acted according to rules . . . The Professor lives under totally extraordinary conditions as it is . . . . We know about his work . . . . We wanted to leave him five whole rooms. . . . Oh, very well . . . If that's the case . . . Very well . . ."

Beet-red, he hung up the receiver and turned around.

That fixed him! What a fellow! the dog thought enthusiastically. He must know some magic word. Now you can thrash me all you want, I'll not leave anyway.

The other three gaped with open mouths at the humiliated Shvonder.

"It's disgraceful!" he mumbled tentatively.

"If we had a discussion now," the woman began, flushing excitedly, "I would prove to Pyotr Alexandrovich . . ."

"Excuse me, you don't intend to open this discussion right now?" Philip Philippovich inquired civilly.

The woman's eyes flared.

"I understand your irony, Professor, we shall leave at once. . . . However, as director of the cultural department of the house, I . . ."

"Di-rect-ress," Philip Philippovich corrected her.

"I want to ask you," and she pulled several magazines, vividly colored and wet from the snow, from the bosom of her coat, "to buy several magazines for the benefit of German children. Fifty kopeks apiece."

"I will not," Philip Philippovich answered briefly, glancing at the magazines out of the corner of his eye.

The four faces expressed utter astonishment, and the woman's face turned a cranberry tinge.

"But why do you refuse?"

"I don't want to."

"Don't you sympathize with the German children?"

"I do."

"You stint the money?"

"No."

"Then why?"

"I don't want to."

They were silent.

"You know, Professor," the girl began, with a deep sigh, "if you were not a world celebrity, and if you weren't protected in the most outrageous manner (the fair-haired man tugged at the edge of her jacket, but she brushed him off) by persons whose authority, I am sure, we shall yet look into, you ought to be arrested."

"And what for?" Philip Philippovich inquired with curiosity.

"You are a hater of the proletariat!" the woman declared proudly.

"You are right, I do not like the proletariat," Philip Philippovich agreed sadly and pressed a button. A bell rang somewhere within, and the door into the corridor swung open.

"Zina," called out Philip Philippovich. "You may serve dinner. Will you allow me, gentlemen?"

The four walked out of the study silently. Silently they crossed the office, silently walked the length of the hallway, and the door could be heard closing behind them with a heavy thud.

The dog rose to his hind legs and performed a kind of salaam before Philip Philippovich.

III

Thin slices of salmon and pickled eel were piled on plates adorned with paradisiac flowers and wide black borders. A piece of fine, moist Swiss cheese lay on a heavy board, and near it stood a silver bucket with caviar, set in a bowl of snow. Among the plates stood several slender liqueur glasses and three crystal carafes with liqueurs of different colors. All these objects were arranged on a small marble table, cosily set against a huge sideboard of carved oak filled with glass and silver, which threw off sheaves of light. In the center of the room a table, heavy as a sepulchre, was covered with a white cloth, and on it were two settings, with napkins rolled like papal tiaras, and three dark bottles.

Zina brought in a covered dish with something sizzling in it. The smell from the dish immediately made the dog's mouth fill with thin saliva. The gardens of Semiramide! he thought, and his tail began to hammer on the parquet like a stick.

"Bring them here," Philip Philippovich commanded fiercely. "Doctor Bormenthal, I implore you, forget the caviar. And if you'll listen to good advice, you'll pour us some ordinary Russian vodka instead of English whisky."

The stunningly handsome bitten one—he was no longer wearing a smock, but an elegant black suit—

31

shrugged his wide shoulders, and poured the transparent liquid with a courteous smile.

"Newly blessed?" he inquired.

"Heaven forbid, my friend," responded the host. "Spirits. Darya Petrovna makes an excellent vodka."

"But why, Philip Philippovich, everybody says it's quite good, eighty-proof."

"And vodka should be ninety-proof, not eighty. That's one," Philip Philippovch interrupted didactically. "And two, heaven knows what they slop into it. Wouldn't you say—whatever comes into their heads?"

"Anything you can name," the bitten one confirmed in a positive tone.

"I am of the same opinion," said Philip Philippovich, throwing the contents down his throat in a single gulp. "Ww . . . Mm . . . Doctor Bormenthal, I beg you: taste this, at once, and if you say—what's this?—I'll be your deadly enemy for the rest of my life. From Seville and to Granada . . ."

With these words, he picked up with his broad-tined silver fork something resembling a tiny dark loaf of bread. The bitten one followed his example. Philip Philippovich's eyes lit up.

"Now, is that bad?" he asked, chewing. "Answer me, my dear Doctor, is it bad?"

"Incomparable," the nipped one responded wholeheartedly.

"Indeed, it is . . . . Mark you, Ivan Arnoldovich, it's only the few remaining landowners whom the Bolsheviks hadn't got around to slaughtering who dine on cold cuts and soup. No self-respecting man will operate with anything but hot dishes. And among Moscow's hot specialties, this is the best. The Slavyansky Market was famous for it once upon a time. Here, catch."

"Feeding the dog in the dining room," a female voice

protested. "You'll never drag him out of here with a
rope after that."

"That's all right. The poor fellow is starved," said
Philip Philippovich offering the dog a tidbit at the end
of his fork. The latter snatched it off with the dexterity
of a juggler, and the fork was flung, clattering, into
the washbasin.

After that, the smell of lobster rose from the steam-
ing plates. The dog sat in the shade of the tablecloth
with the air of a sentry near a powder depot, and
Philip Philippovich, the tail of a crisp napkin stuffed
into his collar, preached:

"Eating, Ivan Arnoldovich, is a cunning art. You
have to know how to eat, and, imagine, most people
haven't the slightest notion of it. It's not only a matter
of knowing what to eat, but also when, and how. (Philip Philippovich wagged his spoon significantly.) And
also what to talk about while you are at it. Yes . . . If
you care about your digestion, my good advice is—do
not talk about Bolshevism or medicine at dinner. And
—heaven preserve!—don't read any Soviet newspapers
before dinner."

"Hm . . . But there are no others."

"That's just it, don't read any. You know, I carried
out thirty tests at my hospital. And what do you think?
Patients who read no newspapers feel excellent. But
those whom I deliberately compelled to read *Pravda*
lost weight."

"Hm . . ." the nipped one responded with interest,
turning pink from the soup and the wine.

"But that isn't all. They had lowered knee-tap re-
flex, rotten appetite, a depressed state of mind."

"The devil, you don't say . . ."

"Oh, yes. But what am I doing? I've started on
medicine myself."

Philip Philippovich leaned back and rang, and Zina appeared from behind the cherry-red hanging. The dog was given a pale, thick slice of sturgeon, which he did not like, and directly after that, a slice of bloody roast beef. Gulping it down, the dog suddenly felt that he must sleep and that he could not bear the sight of any more food. What a strange sensation, he thought, closing his heavy eyelids, I couldn't look at food now. And smoking after dinner is just stupid.

The dining room was filled with unpleasant blue smoke. The dog dozed with his head on his front paws.

"St. Julien is a decent wine," he heard through his sleep, "but where can you get it nowadays?"

The sound of choral singing came from somewhere above, muffled, muted by ceilings and rugs.

Philip Philippovich rang and Zina came in.

"Zinusha, what does this mean?"

"They're having another general meeting, Philip Philippovich," answered Zina.

"Again!" Philip Philippovich exclaimed hopelessly. "Well, it's begun, it's the end of the Kalabukhov house. I'll have to go, but where, I ask you? From now on, the course is clear. First there will be singing every evening, then the pipes in the toilets will freeze, then the boiler will crack—no more steam heat, and so on. Kalabukhov is finished."

"Philip Philippovch is fretting," Zina observed, smiling, as she carried out a pile of dishes.

"But how can you help it?" wailed Philip Philippovich. "What a house this was, if you only knew, what a house!"

"You take too dark a view of things, Philip Philippovich," said the handsome bitten one. "They have changed quite a lot lately."

"My dear friend, you know me, don't you? I am a man of facts, a man of observation. I am an enemy of unfounded hypotheses. And this is well known not only in Russia, but also in Europe. If I say something, you may be sure it is based on certain facts, from which I have drawn conclusions. And here are the facts for you: the coat rack and the stand for galoshes in our house."

"That's interesting . . ."

Such rot—galoshes. Galoshes aren't the main thing, thought the dog. But he's an outstanding personage, no question of that.

"There you are—the stand for galoshes. I have lived in this house since 1903. And throughout all these years, until March, 1917, there was not a single instance—and I underline this with a red pencil, *not a single instance*—of even one pair of galoshes missing from our front hall, with the door always unlocked. And remember, there are twelve apartments here, and I have patients. Well, one fine day in March of 1917, all the galoshes disappeared, including two pair of mine. Also three canes, a coat, and the porter's samovar. And from that day on the stand for galoshes ceased to exist. My dear friend! I won't even mention the steam heat. I won't. Let's forget it: when there's a social revolution, there's no need for steam heat. But I ask you why, when this whole business started, did everyone begin to go up the marble staircase in muddy galoshes and felt boots? Why is it necessary to this day to lock up the galoshes? And even to post a soldier to make sure no one steals them? Why was the rug removed from the front stairway? Does Karl Marx forbid rugs on the stairs? Does he say anywhere in his writings that the second entrance of the Kalabukhov house on Prechistenka must be boarded up, and people must go around the house and enter through the backyard? Who needs this? Why can't the proletarian leave his galoshes downstairs instead of tracking up the marble?"

"But, Philip Philippovich, he doesn't even own any galoshes," the nipped one ventured.

"Nothing of the kind!" Philip Philippovich thundered, pouring himself a glass of wine. "Hm . . . I am against liqueurs after dinner—they make you feel heavy and affect your liver . . . . No such thing! He wears galoshes now, and these galoshes are . . . mine! They are precisely the galoshes which disappeared in the spring of 1917. And I will ask you—who filched them? I? Impossible. The bourgeois Sablin? (Philip Philippovich pointed his finger at the ceiling.) Ridiculous. The sugar manufacturer Polozov? (Philip Philippovich pointed sideways.) Never! Yes, sir! But at least if they would take them off downstairs! (Philip Philippovich began to turn purple.) Why the devil did they remove the plants from the landings? Why is it that the electricity which, if my memory serves me, had gone out twice in twenty years now regularly goes out once a month? Dr. Bormenthal, statistics are a dreadful thing. You, who are familiar with my latest work, know this better than anyone else."

"It's the general rack and ruin, Philip Philippovich. Economic collapse."

"No," Philip Philippovich argued with utmost assurance. "No. You ought to be the first, Ivan Arnoldovich, to refrain from using these terms. They are a mirage, a puff of smoke, a fiction." Philip Philippovich spread out his short fingers, and two shadows like turtles stirred on the tablecloth. "What is this general ruin of yours? An old crone with a crutch? A witch who has knocked out all the windows and extinguished all the lights? Why, there's no such thing! It doesn't exist. What do you mean by these words?" Philip Philippovich addressed himself furiously to the hapless cardboard duck which hung upside down next to the sideboard, and answered for it himself. "It's this: if I

begin to sing in chorus in my apartment every evening
instead of operating, it will lead to ruin. If, coming
into the bathroom, I will—forgive the expression—begin to urinate past the toilet bowl, and if Zina and
Darya Petrovna do the same, I'll have ruin in my bathroom. Hence, the rack and ruin are not in the bathrooms,
but in the heads. And consequently, when these clowns
begin to shout, 'Fight economic ruin!' I must laugh.
(Philip Philippovich's face was so twisted with rage
that the bitten one's mouth dropped open.) I swear to
you, it's funny! It means that everyone of them should
whip himself on the head! And when he knocks all the
hallucinations out of it and begins to clean up the barns
—which is his job in the first place—the general ruin
will disappear of itself. It is impossible to serve two
gods! It is impossible at one and the same time to
sweep the streetcar tracks and settle the fate of Span-
ish beggars! No one can succeed in this, Doctor, and
least of all people who, being generally behind Euro-
peans by some two hundred years, still aren't too sure
of how to button their own pants!"

Philip Philippovich was in a frenzy of excitement.
His hawklike nostrils flared. Reinforced by the hearty
dinner, he thundered like an ancient prophet, and his
head glittered with silver.

His words fell upon the sleepy dog like a dull sub-
terranean hum. The owl with stupid yellow eyes leaped
out at him in his dream; then the vile physiognomy of
the cook in the dirty white cap; then Philip Philippovich's dashing mustache; then a sleepy sled creaked
and vanished, while the ravaged piece of roast beef,
swimming in juice, was being digested in the canine
stomach.

He could earn lots of money at meetings, the dog
dreamed mistily. A first-rate business mind. But he evidently has plenty as it is. "Police!" shouted Philip

Philippovich. "Police!" Oohoo-hoo-hoo! bubbles seemed to burst in the dog's brain . . . .

"Police! That and only that. And it is entirely immaterial whether they have badges or red caps. Post a policeman next to every man and order him to subdue the vocal impulses of our citizens. General collapse, you say? I will tell you, Doctor, that nothing will change for the better in our house, or in any other house, until these singers are quieted down! As soon as they stop their concerts, the situation will take a turn for the better by itself."

"You're saying counterrevolutionary things, Philip Philippovich," the nipped one remarked jocularly. "Heaven forbid if anyone should hear you."

"Nothing dangerous at all," Philip Philippovich countered heatedly. "Nothing counterrevolutionary. And, incidentally, that's another word I can't endure. It's absolutely impossible to tell what it covers! The devil take it! And so, I say: there isn't any of this counterrevolution in my words. There is only common sense and good advice based on practical experience."

Philip Philippovich removed the tail of the shiny, crumpled napkin from behind his collar and, crushing it, put it down next to his unfinished glass of wine. The bitten one immediately rose and thanked him. "Merci."

"One moment, Doctor!" Philip Philippovich stopped him, taking a wallet from his trouser pocket. He squinted, counted off some white notes, and held them out to the bitten one with the words: "Today, Ivan Arnoldovich, you get forty rubles. Please."

The dog's victim thanked him civilly and, blushing, stuffed the money into the pocket of his jacket.

"Will you need me this evening, Philip Philippovich?" he asked.

"No, thank you, my dear. We shall not do anything today. In the first place, the rabbit died. And, in the second, there's *Aida* at the Bolshoi tonight. And I haven't heard it for a long time. I love it . . . . Remember? The duet . . . Tari-rarim."

"How do you manage it all, Philip Philippovich?" the doctor asked with respect.

"He who does not hurry manages to get everywhere," the host explained sententiously. "Of course, if I began to skip around from meeting to meeting and sing all day like a nightingale instead of doing my own work, I would never manage to get anywhere." The repeater watch sang out in heavenly tones under Philip Philippovich's fingers in his pocket. "It's just past eight . . . I'll get there for the second act . . . . I am an advocate of the division of labor. Let them sing at the Bolshoi, and I will operate. Then everything will be fine. And there will be no ruin . . . . And also, Ivan Arnoldovich, do keep your eyes open: as soon as there is a suitable death, straight from the table into a nutrient medium, and rush it here!"

"Don't worry, Philip Philippovich, the pathologists promised me."

"Excellent, and in the meantime we shall observe this stray neurotic and get him into shape. Let his side heal . . . ."

He's concerned about me, thought the dog. A very good man. I know who he is. He is a wizard, a magician, and sorcerer out of a dog's fairy tale . . . I couldn't be dreaming all of this. But what if it is a dream? (The dog started in his sleep.) What if I wake up . . . and there is nothing? No lamp with a silk shade, no warmth, no full stomach. Again the gateway, the fierce cold, the icy pavement, hunger, vicious people . . . the cafeteria, snow . . . God, how bitter it will be! . . .

But nothing of the kind happened. It was the gateway that melted away like an evil dream, never to return.

Evidently, the rack and ruin were not so terrible after all. Despite them, the gray accordions under the windows filled with heat twice daily, and the warmth spread in waves throughout the apartment.

It was quite clear: the dog had pulled out the best dog-ticket. His eyes filled with tears of gratitude to the Prechistenka sage at least twice daily. Besides, all the mirrors in the waiting room and in the office between the cabinets reflected the lucky dog—a real beauty.

I'm a handsome devil. Am I perhaps an unknown canine prince—incognito, the dog wondered, gazing at the shaggy coffee-colored dog with a well-pleased muzzle wandering about in the depths of the mirrors. It is very possible that my grandmother had sinned with a Newfoundland. Look at that white spot on my chin. Where does it come from, I ask you? Philip Philippovich is a man of excellent taste—he wouldn't pick up just any stray mutt.

In the course of a week, the dog gobbled down as much food as he had eaten during the last hungry month and a half in the street. But, of course, measured by weight only. The quality of his present diet was beyond comparison. Even aside from the pile of scraps bought daily by Darya Petrovna at the Smolensk Market for eighteen kopeks, it would be enough to mention the 7 o'clock dinners in the dining room, at which the dog was present despite the protests of the exquisite Zina. During those dinners, Philip Philippovich irrevocably earned the status of divinity. The dog stood up on his hind legs and chewed his jacket. The dog learned to recognize his master's ring—two loud, short blasts —and flew out barking to welcome him in the hallway. The master would tumble in, wrapped in his silver fox glittering with a million snow-sparks, smelling of tangerines, cigars, perfume, lemons, benzine, eau de Cologne, and woolen cloth, and his voice, like a megaphone, resounded through all the rooms.

"You swine, why did you tear the owl to shreds? Was it in your way? Was it, I ask you? Why did you smash Professor Mechnikov?"

"He should be whipped at least once, Philip Philippovich," Zina cried indignantly. "He'll get completely out of hand. Look what he did to your galoshes."

"Nobody should be whipped," Philip Philippovich cried heatedly. "Remember that, once and for all. Neither man nor animal can be influenced by anything but suggestion. Was he given his meat today?"

"Heavens, he's eating us out of house and home. Why do you ask such things, Philip Philippovich. I only wonder why he doesn't burst."

"Well, let him eat all he wants . . . . What did you have against the owl, eh, rascal?"

Ooo-oo! whimpered the fawning dog and crawled on his belly, with his paws splayed out.

Then he was dragged noisily by the scruff of the neck across the waiting room to the office. The dog whimpered, snapped, clutched at the rug with his nails, rode on his backside, like a circus dog. In the middle of the office, on the rug, lay the glassy-eyed owl with a slit belly, from which protruded some red rags smelling of naphthalene. On the table lay the portrait bust, shattered to pieces.

"I deliberately did not tidy up, just so you could admire it," Zina reported excitedly. "He jumped on the table, the scoundrel! and snapped at the tail! Before I knew it, he gutted it. Poke his snout into the owl, Philip Philippovich, let him know how to spoil things."

And a wild howling broke out. The dog, who clung to

the rug, was dragged to have his nose poked at the owl, and he wept bitter tears, praying, beat me, but don't kick me out of here.

"Send the owl to the taxidermist at once. And here is eight rubles and sixteen kopeks for carfare. Go to Muir's and buy him a good collar and chain."

On the following day they put a wide, shiny collar around the dog's neck. At the first moment, as he looked into the mirror, he was dreadfully upset and slunk off to the bathroom with his tail between his legs, wondering how to scrape it off against a trunk or box. But very soon it dawned on him that he was simply being stupid. Zina took him walking on the chain along Obukhov Lane. In the beginning, he walked like a convict, burning up with shame. However, by the time they had reached the Church of Christ on the Prechistenka, he began to realize how much a collar meant in life. There was fierce envy in the eyes of all the dogs he met. And near Dead Man's Alley some rangy mutt with a chopped-off tail barked insults at him, calling him "gentleman's scum" and "six-legs." As they were crossing the streetcar tracks, the militiaman looked at his collar with admiration and respect, and when they returned, the most unheard of thing occurred: Fyodor the doorman opened the front door with his own hands and let Sharik in. And he remarked to Zina, "Look at that shaggy beast Philip Philippovich has gotten himself. And how fat!"

"I'll say! He eats enough for six," said Zina, flushed and pretty from the cold.

A collar is just like a briefcase, the dog quipped mentally and, wagging his behind, proceeded with a lordly air up to the second floor.

Having assessed the full value of a collar, the dog made his first visit to the chief department of paradise, from which he had been categorically banned until then, namely, the realm of the cook, Darya Petrovna. The whole apartment wasn't worth two spans of Darya's kingdom. Every day the stove, black on top and faced with tile, roared and stormed with flames. The oven crackled. In the shafts of scarlet light, Darya Petrovna's face burned with eternal fiery torment and unquenched passion. Her glossy face dripped fat. In her fair hair, fashionably drawn over the ears and formed into a basket in the back, shone twenty-two fake diamonds. Golden saucepans gleamed on hooks along the walls. The entire kitchen clattered with odors, gurgled and hissed with covered pots . . . .

"Out!" shrieked Darya Petrovna. "Out, you homeless sneak thief! All I need is to have you here! I'll bash you with a poker! . . ."

Oh, don't! Why are you scolding? The dog squinted at her with melting eyes. What sort of a sneak thief am I? Don't you see the collar? And he sidled to the door, prying it open with his muzzle.

Sharik possessed some secret power over human hearts. Two days later he was already lying next to the coalbin and watching Darya Petrovna work. With a sharp, narrow knife she chopped off the heads and claws of helpless grouse, then, like a furious executioner, she pulled the soft flesh off the bones, tore the entrails out of chickens, busily turned the meat grinder. And throughout all this, Sharik was torturing a grouse head. Darya Petrovna extracted pieces of roll soaked in milk from a bowl, mixed them with the meat pulp on a board, poured cream over the mixture, salted it, and molded it into patties. The stove hummed like a house on fire, and in the frying pan something gurgled, bubbled and leaped. The door of the oven sprang back with a clatter, revealing a terrifying hell in which flames roared and flashed.

In the evening the fiery maw went dark, and in the

kitchen window, over the white curtain covering the lower panes, stood the dense and dignified Prechistenka night, lit by a solitary star. The kitchen floor was damp, the pans glinted dimly and mysteriously, and a fireman's cap rested on the table. Sharik lay on the warm stove like a lion on a gate and, cocking an ear with curiosity, watched a black-mustachioed, excited man in a wide leather belt embrace Darya Petrovna in the room she shared with Zina. The woman's face burned with torment and passion—all of it, except the dead-white, powdered nose. A crack of light fell on the black-mustachioed man's photograph, with an Easter rose hung over it.

"Pesters me like a demon," muttered Darya Petrovna in the dusk. "Let go! Zina will be here in a minute. What's the matter with you, as though you'd been rejuvenated too?"

"We have no need of it," the mustachioed one spoke huskily, scarcely able to control himself. "How fiery you are!"

Later on in the evening, the Prechistenka star disappeared behind the heavy drawn curtains, and if the Bolshoi did not present *Aida* and there was no meeting of the Russian Surgical Society, the godhead sat in a deep chair in his office. There were no ceiling lights, only the green-shaded lamp on the table. Sharik lay in the shadow on the rug and looked, unblinking, at terrible doings. In a disgusting, caustic, muddy liquid in glass containers lay human brains. The godhead's hands, bared to the elbow, were dressed in reddish rubber gloves, and the slippery, blunt fingers fumbled in the convolutions. From time to time, the godhead armed himself with a small gleaming knife and carefully cut into the firm yellow brains.

"To the sacred banks of the Nile," the godhead sang quietly, then bit his lips, recalling the golden interior of the Bolshoi Theatre.

At this hour the heat in the radiators reached its highest point. It rose to the ceiiing and thence spread through the room. In the dog's fur, the last flea, not yet combed out by Philip Philippovich himself, but already doomed, awakened. The front door clanked distantly.

Zina went to the movies, the dog thought. And when she returns, we shall have supper. I guess we'll have veal cutlets today!

IV

Already in the morning of that dreadful day Sharik
had had a pang of premonition. He suddenly whimpered, and ate his breakfast—half a cup of gruel and last
night's lamb bone—without appetite. Dismally, he
walked to the waiting room and howled a little at his
own reflection. But after Zina had taken him for a
walk on the boulevard, the day passed as usual. There
were no visitors, since, as everyone knew, Tuesdays
were not visiting days, and the godhead sat at the desk
in his office, poring over some huge volumes with
brightly colored pictures. They waited for dinner.
The dog was slightly cheered by the thought that they
would have turkey for the second course, as he had
learned in the kitchen. As he walked down the hall, he
heard the sudden unpleasant ringing of the telephone
in Philip Philippovich's office. Philip Philippovich
picked up the receiver, listened, and suddenly became
excited.

"Excellent," his voice was saying. "Bring it over at
once, at once!"

He started bustling, rang, and ordered Zina to serve
dinner without delay.

"Dinner! Dinner! Dinner!"

Plates immediately began to clatter in the dining
room, Zina hurried back and forth, and in the kitchen

Darya Petrovna grumbled that the turkey was not yet ready. The dog felt a twinge of anxiety again.

I hate commotion in the house, the dog thought . . . And just as he said it to himself, the commotion assumed an even more unpleasant character, chiefly thanks to the arrival of the once-nipped Dr. Bormenthal. The latter brought with him an evil smelling suitcase and, neglecting to remove his coat, hurried with it along the hallway to the examination room. Philip Philippovich abandoned his unfinished cup of coffee, which he had never done before, and ran out to meet Bormenthal, which he had never done either.

"When did he die?" he cried.

"Three hours ago," said Bormenthal, without removing his snow-covered hat and unlocking the suitcase.

Who died? the dog wondered with glum annoyance and got in their way. I can't stand all this fuss.

"Get out from underfoot! Hurry, hurry, hurry!" shouted Philip Philippovich in all directions, and began, it seemed to the dog, to ring all the bells. Zina came running. "Zina! Send Darya Petrovna to the telephone to take down the calls. Admit no one! You'll be needed. Dr. Bormenthal, I implore you—hurry, hurry, hurry!"

I don't like it, I don't like it at all, the dog frowned offendedly and went wandering over the apartment, while all the excitement was concentrated in the examination room. Zina was suddenly wearing a smock that looked like a shroud, and began to run back and forth between examination room and kitchen.

Guess I'll go and eat something. To hell with them all, decided the dog, when he suddenly got a surprise.

"Don't feed Sharik," thundered the order from the examination room.

"Hm, try and keep him from food!"

"Lock him up!"

And Sharik was lured into the bathroom and locked up.

The swine, thought Sharik, sitting in the dim bathroom. Stupid . . .

And he spent about fifteen minutes in the bathroom in the strangest mood—now furious, now falling into an odd, heavy apathy. Everything was depressing, unclear . . . .

All right, my most esteemed Philip Philippovich, see what happens to your galoshes tomorrow, he thought. You've had to buy two new pair, you'll buy a third one now. That will teach you to lock up dogs.

But suddenly his angry thoughts broke off. For some reason, a vivid fragment of his earliest youth rose in his memory: a vast, sunny courtyard near the Preobrazhensky Turnpike, splinters of sun in bottles, cracked bricks, free, stray dogs.

Oh, no, why lie to yourself, you'll never leave here, you'll never go back to freedom, the dog spoke to himself in anguish, sniffling. I am a gentleman's dog, an intellectual creature, I've tasted a better life. And what is freedom, anyway? Nothing, a puff of smoke, a mirage, a fiction . . . A sick dream of those wretched democrats . . .

Then the dusk of the bathroom became terrifying. He howled, threw himself at the door, began to scratch at it.

Oo-oo-oo! the apartment echoed like a barrel. I'll tear that owl again, the dog thought with impotent fury. Then he collapsed, exhausted, rested a while, and when he rose, his fur suddenly bristled on his back: it seemed to him for a moment that he saw a pair of loathsome wolf's eyes in the bathtub.

At the height of his torment, the door swung open. The dog came out, shook himself, and gloomily turned toward the kitchen, but Zina insistently dragged him by the collar to the examination room. A chill crept under the dog's heart.

What do they need me for? he thought suspiciously. My side is healed. I don't understand anything.

His paws slithered on the shiny parquet, and it was thus that he was dragged into the examination room. He was immediately struck by the unusual illumination. The white sphere under the ceiling gleamed so brightly that it hurt the eyes. In the white blaze stood a priest who hummed through his teeth about the sacred banks of the Nile. Nothing but a vague smell indicated that this was Philip Philippovich. His cropped gray hair was hidden under a white cap, resembling a patriarch's cowl. The godhead was in white from head to foot, and over it, like a scapular, he wore a narrow, rubber apron. His hands were hidden in black gloves.

The bitten one was also in the cupola of light. The long table was extended, and near it stood a little square one on a gleaming leg.

Most of all in this room, the dog hated the bitten one, and mostly because of his eyes—usually bold and direct, today they ran in all directions, evading the dog's eyes. They were guarded, false, and held in their depths something nasty, evil, something criminal. The dog gave him a glum and heavy look and slunk off into a corner.

"The collar, Zina," Philip Philippovich said in an undertone. "But don't excite him."

Zina's eyes immediately became as vile as the bitten one's. She approached the dog and gave him an obviously false pat. He looked at her with anguish and contempt.

Well . . . There are three of you. You'll get me, if you want to. But shame on you . . . At least, if I only knew what you're going to do to me . . . .

Zina undid the collar; the dog shook his head, snorting. The nipped one appeared before him, spreading a foul, nauseating smell.

Ugh, disgusting . . . Why do I feel so sick and frightened? . . . the dog thought, backing away.

"Hurry up, Doctor," Philip Philippovich said impatiently.

The air filled with a sharp, sweetish odor. The bitten one, fixing the dog with his watchful, rotten eyes, took his right hand from behind his back and qu-kly slapped a piece of damp cotton over the dog's nose. Sharik was stunned, his head reeled slightly, but he still had time to recoil. The bitten one jumped after him, and suddenly covered his whole muzzle with the cotton. His breath stopped, but the dog still managed to break away once more. Murderer . . . flashed in his head. Why? What for? And once again the cotton covered his nose and mouth. Suddenly there was a lake in the middle of the examination room, and on it jolly oarsmen in boats—extraordinary pink dogs. His legs became boneless, and buckled.

"On the table," Philip Philippovich's words boomed out somewhere gaily and spread in orange-colored rivulets. The terror vanished, giving place to joy. For two seconds the expiring dog loved the nipped one. Then the whole world turned upside down, and he felt a cold but pleasant hand under his belly. And then—nothing.

The dog Sharik lay sprawled out on the narrow operating table, and his head helplessly knocked against the white oilcloth cushion. His belly was shaved and now Dr. Bormenthal, breathing heavily and hurrying, was shaving Sharik's head, the clipper chewing into the fur. Philip Philippovich leaned against the edge of the table, watching the procedure with eyes that glittered like the gold rims of his glasses. He said excitedly:

"Ivan Arnoldovich, the most important moment is when I enter the Turkish saddle. I implore you, hand me the pituitary instantly—it must be sewed on at once. If bleeding begins there, we shall lose time and lose the dog. Not that he has a chance, anyway." He was silent, squinted, and, with a seemingly mocking glance into the dog's half-closed eye, added, "But, you know, I feel sorry for him. Imagine, I've gotten used to him."

His hands were raised all this time, as though blessing the luckless mongrel Sharik for a heroic feat. He was trying to keep his black gloves free of a single speak of dust.

The dog's whitish skin gleamed from under the shaved fur. Bormenthal flung away the clippers and armed himself with a razor. He soaped the small helpless head and began to shave it. The razor scraped loudly, and here and there a drop of blood appeared. When he had finished shaving, the bitten one wiped the head with a wad of cotton dipped in alcohol. Then he stretched the dog's bare belly and said, puffing, "Ready."

Zina opened the faucet over the sink and Bormenthal hurried over to wash his hands. Zina poured alcohol on them from a bottle.

"May I go, Philip Philippovich?" she asked, fearfully squinting at the dog's shaved head.

"You may go."

Zina disappeared. Bormenthal busied himself further. He spread light napkins around Sharik's head, and now the two men beheld the unprecedented sight of a bald canine head and strange bearded muzzle resting on the cushion.

The priest stirred. He drew himself up, glanced at the dog's head, and said:

"Well, with God's blessing. Knife."

Bormenthal took a small potbellied knife from the gleaming pile on the little table and handed it to the priest. Then he put on black gloves, similar to the priest's.

"Sleeping?" said Philip Philippovich.

"Fast asleep."

Philip Philippovich clenched his teeth, his little eyes acquired a piercing, prickly glitter. He swung the knife and made a sharp, long incision on Sharik's belly. The skin parted at once and blood spurted in all directions. Bormenthal rushed in fiercely and began to press Sharik's wound with wads of gauze. Then he clipped the edges together with tiny instruments that looked like sugar tongs, and the wound dried out. Perspiration came out in beads on Bormenthal's forehead. Philip Philippovich slashed Sharik a second time, and together they began to tear his body apart with hooks, scissors, clips. Pink and yellow tissues jumped out, weeping with bloody dew. Philip Philippovich turned the knife in the body, then cried, "Scissors!"

The instrument flashed in the bitten one's hands as if he were a sleight-of-hand artist. Philip Philippovich plunged his hand deep into the belly and, with a few twists, tore out of Sharik's body his seminal vesicles, with some shreds hanging from them. Bormenthal, wet with effort and excitement, rushed to the glass jar and drew from it another set of moist and drooping seminal vesicles. Short, moist threads whirled and jumped in the hands of the professor and his assistant. Curved needles chattered rapidly against the clips, and the vesicles were sewn in, in place of Sharik's original ones. The priest threw himself back from the wound, stuck a piece of gauze into it, and commanded:

"Sew up the skin, Doctor, instantly." Then he looked back at the round white clock on the wall.

"Fourteen minutes," Bormenthal hissed out through clenched teeth, and drove the curved needle into the flabby skin. Then both became as frantic as hurrying murderers.

"Knife," cried Philip Philippovich.

The knife leaped into his hands as of its own volition, and Philip Philippovich's face became awe-inspiring. His lips drew back from his porcelain and gold caps, and with a single sweep he carved a red crown on Sharik's forehead. The shaven skin was thrown back like a scalp. The skull was bared. Philip Philippovich shouted, "Trepan!"

Bormenthal handed him a shiny brace. Biting his lips, Philip Philippovich began to force the bit into Sharik's skull and drill in it tiny holes a centimeter apart, so that they formed a circle all around the skull. He spent no more than five seconds on each hole. Then with an oddly shaped saw, the end of which he inserted into the first hole, he began to saw, just as a cabinetmaker would saw a lady's sewing chest. The skull shook and squeaked. Three minutes later the lid was removed from Sharik's skull.

The cupola of Sharik's brain was bared—gray, with bluish veins and reddish spots. Philip Philippovich plunged the scissors into the meninges and cut them away. Once a thin spurt of blood shot out, almost striking the professor in the eye and spotting his cap. Bormenthal pounced like a tiger with a torsion forceps and shut it off. Sweat crept down his face in rivulets, and the face became meaty and varicolored. His eyes dashed from the professor's hands to the bowl with instruments on the table, then back. And Philip Philippovich became positively terrifying. He snorted through his nose, his teeth were bared to the gums. He tore the sheath from the brain and delved somewhere deep, raising the cerebral hemispheres out of the opened cavity. At this point, Bormenthal began to turn pale. He grasped Sharik's chest with one hand and said hoarsely:

"The pulse is falling sharply. . . ."

Philip Philippovich threw him a vicious glance, mumbled something, and cut still deeper. Bormenthal cracked a glass ampule, sucked out the contents with a syringe and treacherously stuck the needle somewhere near Sharik's heart.

"I'm coming to the Turkish saddle," Philip Philippovich growled, and lifted Sharik's grayish-yellow brain from the skull. For a moment he squinted at Sharik's muzzle, and Bormenthal instantly broke a second ampule with yellow liquid and drew it into a long syringe.

"Into the heart?" he asked timidly.

"You're asking?" the professor roared furiously. "He has died five times already in your hands, anyway. Inject it! Impossible!" And his face assumed the expression of an inspired cutthroat.

The doctor plunged the needle into the dog's heart easily.

"Alive, but just barely," he whispered diffidently.

"No time for discussion now—alive, not alive," the terrifying Philip Philippovich hissed. "I'm in the saddle. He'll die anyway . . . Ah, the dev . . . Toward the sacred . . . Pituitary, here."

Bormenthal handed him a jar with fluid in which a little white lump dangled on a thread. With one hand ("By God . . . he has no equal in Europe!" Bormenthal thought vaguely) he seized the dangling lump, and with the other, somewhere in the depths between the outspread hemispheres, he sheared out a similar one. He flung Sharik's lump away into a plate, and inserted the new one in the brain, together with its thread. Then his short fingers, which had become, as by a miracle, thin and nimble, had managed cunningly to tie it in place with an amber thread. After that he threw out of the head all sorts of clips and forceps, pushed the brain back into the skull cavity, leaned back, and asked more calmly:

"He's dead, of course? . . ."

"Thready pulse," said Bormenthal.

"More adrenalin."

The professor threw the meninges back over the brain, carefully replaced the sawed-out lid, pulled back the scalp, and roared, "Stitch!"

Bormenthal sewed up the head in some five minutes, breaking three needles.

And now, against the bloodstained background of the cushion, there appeared Sharik's extinguished, lifeless muzzle with a circular wound on his head. Philip Philippovich fell back from the table like a satiated vampire, tore off one glove, sending up a cloud of sweaty powder, ripped the other, flung it on the floor, and pressing the button in the wall, rang. Zina appeared on the threshold, turning her face away from the bloodied Sharik. The priest removed his bloodstained cowl with chalky hands and shouted:

"A cigarette, Zina, at once. Fresh underwear, and a bath."

He rested his chin on the edge of the table, spread open the dog's right eyelids with two fingers, glanced into the obviously dying eye, and said:

"The devil take it. He didn't die. Oh, well, he'll die anyway. Ah, Doctor Bormenthal, I'm sorry for the mutt. He was sly, but affectionate."

V

Laboratory dog, approximately two years old. Male.
Breed—mongrel. Name—Sharik. Fur—thin, shaggy,
grayish brown, mottled. Tail, color of boiled milk.
Traces of healed burns on the left side. Undernourished
before coming to professor; after a week's stay, very
solid, in good condition. Weight—8 kilograms (ex-
clamation point). Heart, lungs, stomach, temperature . . .

December 23. At 8:15 P.M.—first operation in Europe according to Prof. Preobrazhensky: Sharik's
testes removed under chloroform anesthesia and replaced by graft of human testes with epididymis and
seminal cords, obtained from a man of twenty-eight
who died four hours and four minutes before the
operation and preserved in sterile physiological fluid
according to Prof. Preobrazhensky.

Directly following, pituitary gland, or hypophysis,
removed after trepanning of skull and replaced by a
human one taken from above man.

Expended: 8 cubes of chloroform, 1 syringe of camphor, 2 syringes of adrenalin into the heart.

Operative indications: Preobrazhensky experiment
with combined transplantation of hypophysis and testes
to determine viability of hypophysis transplant and,

subsequently, its effect on rejuvenation of human organism.

Operation performed by Prof. P. P. Preobrazhensky. Assisted by Dr. I. A. Bormenthal.

Night following operation: repeated dangerous decline of pulse rate. Fatal outcome expected. Huge doses of camphor according to Preobrazhensky.

December 24. Morning—improvement. Respiration rate doubled, temperature 42°C. Camphor, caffeine injected subcutaneously.

December 25. Deterioration again. Pulse still perceptible. Extremities cold, no reaction in pupils. Adrenalin into heart, camphor according to Preobrazhensky, physiological solution injected intravenously.

December 26. Slight improvement. Pulse 180, respiration 92, temperature 41. Camphor, alimentation by enema.

December 27. Pulse 152, respiration 50, temperature 39.8, pupils reacting. Camphor subcutaneously.

December 28. Significant improvement. Sudden drenching sweat at noon. Temperature 37. Operational wounds in the same condition. Change of dressing. Appearance of appetite. Liquid diet.

December 29. Sudden shedding of fur on forehead and sides of body. Invited for consultation: Professor of Dermatology Vasily Vasilievich Bundarev and director of Moscow Model Veterinary Institute. Consultants declare case unknown in literature. Diagnosis remains undetermined. Temperature—.

(Entry with pencil)

First bark in the evening (8:15). Sharp change of timbre and lowering of tone noted. Instead of "wow-wow" sound, bark consists of syllables, "a-o," remotely reminiscent of moan.

December 30. Falling out of hair assumes character

of progressive general depilation. Weighing-in produced unexpected results: weight 30 kilograms, accounted for by growth (lengthening) of bones. Dog still bedridden.

December 31. Colossal appetite.

(Blot in record book. After blot, in hurried writing)
At 12:12 dog clearly barked "ts-u-rt."

(Break in the book, then, evidently written by mistake in excitement)

December 1. (Crossed out, corrected) January 1, 1925. Photographed this morning. Happily barks "tsurt," repeating the word loudly and apparently gaily. At 3 P.M. *(in large letters)* he laughed, causing the maid Zina to faint. In the evening pronounced eight times the word "tsurt-hsif," "tsurt."

(In slanting writing, in pencil) The professor decoded the word "tsurt-hsif." It means "fish-trust" . . . Something incompre. . .

January 2. Photographed, smiling, by flash. Got out of bed and remained confidently on hind legs half an hour. Almost my height.

(On sheet inserted into book)

Russian science has nearly suffered a grievous loss.

Record of illness of Professor P. P. Preobrazhensky.

At 1:13—deep faint. In falling, Prof. Preobrazhensky struck his head on chair leg.

In the presence of myself and Zina, the dog (if, indeed, one may use this designation) swore obscenely at Prof. Preobrazhensky.

January 6. (Partly in pencil, partly in violet ink)

Today, after his tail dropped off, he enunciated with utmost clarity the word "saloon." The recording machine is working. The devil knows what is going on.

I am totally bewildered.

Professor no longer receives patients. From 5 P.M.
the examination room, where this creature is walking
about, resounds with definitely vulgar oaths and the
words, "another double."

January 7. He says many words: "cabby," "no
room," "evening paper," "the best present for children," and all the oaths and obscenities that exist in
the Russian language.

His appearance is strange. The fur remains only on
his head, chin, and chest. The rest of his body is bald,
with flabby skin. In the genital area—a maturing man.
The skull has grown considerably larger. The forehead
is low and slanting.

I swear, I shall go mad.

Philip Philippovich is still feeling ill. Most of the
observation is done by me. *(Recorder, photographs).*

Rumor spreading in the city.

Innumerable consequences. Today the entire lane
was crowded with idlers and old women. They are still
gaping under our window. The morning papers carried an astonishing item: "The rumors about a Martian in Obukhov Lane are totally unfounded. They
were spread by the peddlers on Sukharevka and will
be severely punished." What Martian, damn them?
It's a nightmare.

Evening Moscow has done still better—it reports
the birth of a baby who plays the violin. This is illus-
trated by a drawing of a violin and my photograph,
with the legend, "Prof. Preobrazhensky, who performed the caesarian operation on the mother." It's

indescribable. . . . He says a new word, "militiaman."

It turns out that Darya Petrovna was in love with me and swiped my photograph from Philip Philippovich's album. After I turned out the reporters, one of them got into the kitchen, etc. . . .

The things that go on during visiting hours! The bell rang eighty-two times today. The telephone was disconnected. Childless ladies have gone berserk and are coming in droves. . . .

The house committee sits in full attendance, with Shvonder presiding. They themselves don't know why.

January 8. Diagnosis established late in the evening. Philip Philippovich, like a true scientist, acknowledged his mistake: a change of hypophysis produces, not rejuvenation, but complete humanization *(underlined three times)*. This does not detract in the slightest from the staggering importance of his amazing discovery.

The creature took his first walk around the apartment. He laughed in the hallway, looking at the electric light. Then, accompanied by Philip Philippovich and myself, he proceeded to the office. He stands firmly on his hind *(last word crossed out)* . . . feet and looks like a short and poorly built man.

He laughed in the office. His smile is unpleasant and seems artificial. Then he scratched his head, looked around, and I wrote down another clearly enunciated word, "bourgeois." Swore. His swearing is methodical, continuous, and apparently entirely senseless. Gives the impression of a phonograph record—as if this creature has heard the oaths somewhere before, has automatically and subconsciously recorded them in his brain, and is now spouting them in batches. But what the devil, I am not a psychiatrist.

For some reason, his swearing elicits an extremely painful reaction in Philip Philippovich. There are moments when he departs from the cool and controlled attitude of an observer of new phenomena and seems to lose patience. Once, during an outburst of oaths, he suddenly shouted nervously:

"Stop it!"

This produced no effect.

After his walk in the study, Sharik was installed by our combined efforts in the examination room.

After that I had a conference with Philip Philippovich. I must admit that this was the first time I saw this self-confident and extraordinarily intelligent man bewildered. Humming his usual tunes, he asked me, "Well, what are we to do now?" And then, answered himself: "Moscow Sewing Industries Trust, yes. . . . From Seville and to Granada. The Moscow Sewing Industries Trust, my dear Doctor. . ." I understood nothing. He explained: "I beg you, Ivan Arnoldovich, buy him some underwear, trousers, and a jacket."

January 9. His vocabulary is enriched every five minutes (on the average) by a new word, and, since this morning, also by entire phrases. It seems as if they had been frozen in his mind, and now they are thawing out and emerging. Every word that emerges remains in use. Last night the recorder noted "don't push," "scoundrel," "get off the step," "I'll show you," "recognition of America," and "primus stove."

January 10. He was dressed. He permitted the undershirt to be put on quite readily, even laughing gaily, but refused the underpants, protesting with hoarse shouts: "Get on line, sons of bitches, get on line!" He was dressed. The socks were too large for him.

(Schematic sketches in the book, evidently showing

the transformation of a dog's foot into a human one.)

The heel of the foot is lengthening. Also toes. Claws. Repeated systematic toilet training. Servants are utterly depressed.

But note must be made of the creature's quick understanding. Situation is rapidly improving.

January 11. He has completely accepted the trousers. Spoke a long, gay phrase: "Let's have a smoke, or I'll give you a poke."

The fur on the head is thin and silky. Can easily be confused with hair. But remains mottled on the crown. Today the last down was shed from the ears. Colossal appetite. Eats herring with great relish.

At 5 P.M., an event: for the first time the creature's words were not dissociated from surrounding facts, but were a direct reaction to them. When the professor told him: "Stop throwing food on the floor," he unexpectedly answered: "Leave me alone, louse."

Philip Philippovich was stunned, then he recovered and said:

"If you permit yourself to insult me or the doctor again, you'll get it."

I photographed Sharik at that moment. I swear that he understood the professor's words. A sullen shadow fell on his face. He gave us a scowling look from under his brow, but became quiet.

Hurrah, he understands!

January 12. Puts his hands in his trouser pockets. We are trying to break him from swearing. He whistled, "Hey, little apple." Takes part in conversation.

I cannot refrain from certain hypotheses. To the devil with rejuvenation for the time being. Something else is immeasurably more important: Prof. Preobrazhensky's amazing experiment has revealed one of the secrets of the human brain. From now on, the mysteri-

ous function of the hypophysis—the brain appendage
—is explained. The hypophysis determines human
characteristics. Its hormones may be described as the
most important ones in the organism—they are the
hormones of the human shape. A new realm is opening
in science: a homunculus was created without any of
Faust's retorts. The surgeon's scalpel has brought into
being a new human entity. Professor Preobrazhensky,
you are a creator. *(Blot)*

However, I have digressed. . . . And so, he maintains
his end of a conversation. My hypothesis is that the
grafted hypophysis has opened a speech center in the
canine brain, and words have burst out in a stream.
In my view, what we see is a resuscitated and expanded
brain, and not a newly created one. Oh, the marvelous
confirmation of the theory of evolution! Oh, the greatest chain of evolution from dog to the chemist Men-
deleyev! And another hypothesis: during his canine
existence, Sharik's brain accumulated a mass of con-
cepts. All the words he used in the beginning were
gutter words. He heard them and stored them in his
brain. Now, as I walk in the street, I look at dogs with
secret horror. Who knows what is hidden in their
heads.

Sharik knew how to read. He read. *(Three exclama-
tion points)* I've guessed it. From "Fish Trust." And
he read from the end. I even know where the solution
to this riddle lies: in the special nature of the dog's
optic nerves.

What is happening in Moscow is inconceivable to
the mind. Seven vendors from the Sukharevka are already in prison for spreading rumors about the end of
the world, brought on by the Bolsheviks. Darya Petrovna told us about it and even gave the exact date:

on November 28, 1925, the day of the martyred St. Stephen, the earth will collide with a heavenly axis. . . . Some charlatans are already giving lectures on the coming of the end. We have unleashed such a circus with this hypophysis that I am afraid we shall have to run from here. I have moved into Preobrazhensky's apartment at his request, and sleep in the waiting room with Sharik. The examination room has been turned into a waiting room. Shvonder turned out to be right. The house committee is gloating. The glass in all the cabinets is broken because he was always jumping. We've barely managed to get him out of the habit.

Something strange is happening to Philip. When I told him about my hypothesis and said that we may develop Sharik into a personality of a high psychic order, he grunted and replied, "You think so?" His tone was ominous. Can it be that I am mistaken? The old man has something up his sleeve. While I am busy with the case history, he is poring over the history of the man from whom we obtained the hypophysis.

(Sheet inserted into the record book)
Klim Grigorievich Chugunkin, twenty-five years old, single. Non-partisan, sympathizer. Arrested and tried three times. Acquitted the first time, because of insufficient evidence; the second time, saved by his social origin; the third time, sentenced to fifteen years at hard labor; released on probation. Thefts. Profession: balalaika player in bars.

Short, poorly built. Enlarged liver (alcohol). Cause of death: struck with a knife in the heart in saloon (The Stop Signal, near the Preobrazhensky Turnpike).

The old man pores steadily over Klim's case history.

I don't understand what it's all about. He mumbled something about my failure to examine Chugunkin's whole body in the pathology laboratory. What is wrong? I cannot understand it. What difference whose hypophysis?

January 17. I have made no entries for several days —was sick with influenza. During these days his characteristics have evolved completely.

a)   Body structure—entirely human.

b)   Weight—approximately 3 poods.

c)   Height—short.

d)   Head—small.

e)   Has begun to smoke.

f)   Eats human food.

g)   Dresses himself without help.

h)   Converses easily.

So much for the hypophysis *(Blot).*

With this, I close the case history. We are before a new organism, requiring a new and separate series of observations.

Appended: stenographic record of speech, phonograph records, photographs.

Signed: Assistant to Prof. P. P. Preobrazhensky,

                              Dr. Bormenthal

VI

It was a winter evening. The end of January. Just before dinner and visiting hours. A white sheet of paper was attached to the frame of the door to the waiting room. It bore several inscriptions. The first, in Philip Philippovich's hand, read:

No eating of sunflower seeds in the apartment.
—P. Preobrazhensky

Under this, with a blue pencil, in huge letters, in Bormenthal's hand:

No playing on musical instruments from
5 P.M. to 7 A.M.

Then, in Zina's hand:

When you return, tell Philip Philippovich that I don't know where he is. Fyodor said he went out with Shvonder.

In Preobrazhensky's hand:

Do I have to wait for the glazier a hundred years?

In Darya Petrovna's hand (*printed letters*):

Zina went to the store, said she would bring him.

The lamp with the cherry-red shade was already lit

in the dining room. The reflection from the sideboard
was broken in half—the plate glass was taped over
with a slanting cross from bevel to bevel. Philip Philippovich, bending over the table, was absorbed in an
enormous, wide-open newspaper. Lightning flashes ran
across his face, and broken, chopped off, smothered
words came droning from behind his teeth. He was
reading a news item:

There is no doubt whatsover that this is his ille-
gitimate son (as they used to say in the corrupt
bourgeois society). This is how our pseudo-scientific
bourgeoisie amuses itself. Anyone can occupy seven
rooms—until the gleaming sword of justice flashes
its scarlet ray over his head.

Shv . . . .r

The very persistent sounds of a balalaika, played
with reckless ease, came from behind two walls, and
the nimble, complicated variations on "The Moon is
Shining" mingled with the words of the news item,
creating a loathsome hodgepodge in Philip Philippovich's head. When he finished reading, he spat drily
over his shoulder and mechanically began to sing
through his teeth:

"The moon is shin-ing. . . The moo-n is. . . The
moon is shining. . . Phew, can't get rid of that damned
tune!"

He rang. Zina's face appeared between the hangings.

"Tell him to stop, it's 5 o'clock, and tell him to come
here, please."

Philip Philippovich sat in his armchair at the table.
Between the fingers of his left hand he held a brown
cigar stub. Near the hanging, a short man of unpleasant appearance stood leaning against the door-jamb,
one leg crossed over the other. The hair on his head
was coarse and stood up like shrubs in a badly cleared

field, and his face was covered with stubble. His forehead was strikingly low. The thick brush of hair began almost directly over the black tufts of his shaggy eyebrows.

Bits of straw clung to his jacket, ripped open under the left arm; the tight striped trousers were torn on the right knee and spotted with lilac paint on the left. Around his neck, the man wore a poisonously blue tie with a fake ruby pin. The color of the tie was so garish that, even when he closed his weary eyes from time to time, Philip Philippovich saw in the total dark, now on the wall and now on the ceiling, a flaming torch with a blue corona. When he opened his eyes, he was blinded again by the glittering fans of light shooting up from the floor from the patent shoes with white spats.

"As though he were wearing galoshes," Philip Philippovich thought irritably. He sighed, snorted and busied himself with relighting his cigar. The man at the door looked at the professor with lacklustre eyes and smoked a cigarette, scattering ash on his shirt front.

The clock on the wall next to the wooden grouse rang five. Something was still groaning inside it when Philip Philippovich opened the conversation.

"I believe that I have asked you twice not to sleep on the bench in the kitchen, especially during the day?"

The man gave a hoarse cough, as though choking on a bone, and answered:

"The air is more pleasant in the kitchen."

His voice was unusual, somewhat flat and yet booming as out of a small barrel.

Philip Philippovich shook his head and asked:

"Where did you get this trash? I mean the tie."

The little man followed the pointing finger with his

eyes, crossed them over his pouting lip, and looked lovingly at the tie."

"Why 'trash'?" he objected. "It's an elegant tie. Darya Petrovna gave me a present."

"Darya Petrovna gave you a piece of abomination, like those shoes of yours. What sort of gleaming nonsense is that? Where did you get them? What did I say? I said they were to buy you de-cent shoes. And what's that? Dr. Bormenthal could not have chosen them."

"I told him patent leather. What am I, worse than anybody else? Go take a look on Kuznetsky Bridge—everybody wears patent."

Philip Philippovich turned his head and said emphatically:

"There will be no more sleeping on the bench. Is that clear? What impertinence! You are in the way. And there are women there."

The man's face darkened and his lips puffed out.

"Women, some women! Imagine. Ladies! Ordinary servants, and putting on airs like commissars' wives. It's all Zinka's squealing."

Philip Philippovich threw him a stern glance:

"Don't dare to call Zina Zinka! Is that clear?"

Silence.

"I'm asking you, is that clear?"

"Clear enough."

"Remove that rag from your neck. You . . . Sha . . . just take a look at yourself in the mirror, see what you look like. A clown. Stop throwing butts on the floor—I ask you for the hundredth time. And no more swearing in the apartment! No spitting! Here is a spittoon. Take care when you use the toilet. Stop all conversation with Zina. She complains that you lie in wait for her in the dark. Look out! Who said to a patient, 'The son of a bitch knows!'? What is this, do you think you are in a saloon?"

"You're getting too hard on me, dad," the man suddenly blubbered.

Philip Philippovich turned red and his glasses flashed.

"Who's your dad here? What kind of familiarity? I never want to hear that word again! Address me by name and patronymic!"

An insolent expression flared up in the man's face.

"Why are you nagging all the time? . . . Don't spit. Don't smoke. Don't go here . . . Don't go there . . . What sort of business is it anyway? Just like in the streetcar. Why'nt you let me live? And as for 'dad,' you've no call to . . . Did I ask you for the operation?" The man barked indignantly. "A fine thing! Grabbed an animal beast, slashed up his head with a knife, and now they're squeamish. Maybe I never gave you no permission to operate? And likewise (the man rolled up his eyes to the ceiling, as though trying to remember a certain formula), and likewise my relatives. I have the right to sue you, maybe."

Philip Philippovich's eyes became completely round, and the cigar dropped out of his hand. "What a character," flashed in his head.

"Is it your pleasure to complain because you have been transformed into a man?" he asked, narrowing his eyes. "Perhaps you prefer to root around in garbage bins again? Freeze in gateways? Well, if I had known . . ."

"Why are you throwing it up all the time—garbage and garbage. I came by my piece of bread honestly. And if I'd died under your knife? What will you say to that, comrade?"

"Philip Philippovich!" Philip Philippovich cried irritably. "I'm no comrade of yours! It's monstrous!" A nightmare, a nightmare, he thought to himself.

"But nach'rally, sure . . ." the man said with irony and put one foot forward triumphantly. "We understand you, Sir. What sort of comrades are we to you! What are we? We didn't study in no universities, we've never lived in fifteen-room apartments with bathrooms. Except it's time to forget all that now. At the present moment everybody has his right. . . ."

Philip Philippovich paled as he listened to the man's harangue. The latter broke off his speech and demonstratively proceeded toward the ash tray with the chewed up cigarette in his hand. He walked with a loose, swinging gait. For a long time he kneaded the butt in the shell with an expression that said unmistakably, "All right! There!" After he put out the cigarette, he suddenly thrust his nose under his arm and clicked his teeth.

"Use your fingers to catch fleas! Your fingers!" Philip Philippovich shouted furiously. "And I don't understand it—where do you get them from?"

"What do you think, I breed them, maybe?" the man was offended. "I guess the fleas like me." He felt with his fingers in the lining under his sleeve, and sent a tuft of light yellow cotton flying in the air.

Philip Philippovich turned up his eyes to the garlands on the ceiling and tapped his fingers on the table. The man executed the flea, walked aside and sat down on a chair, letting his hands hang down from the wrist along the lapels of his coat. His eyes crossed as he looked down on the squares of the parquet. He contemplated his shoes, and this obviously gave him great pleasure. Philip Philippovich glanced at the sharp glints on the blunt toes, closed his eyes and asked:

"What else did you want to tell me?"

"What else! It's a simple business. I need a document, Philip Philippovich."

Philip Philippovich twitched.

"Hm . . . What the devil! A document! Yes, indeed . . . Hmm . . . But perhaps you can somehow do without . . ." his voice was troubled and uncertain.

"But how can you say that," the man replied confidently. "How can you do without documents? Excuse me . . . You know it yourself, a man is strictly forbidden to exist without documents. In the first place, the house committee. . . ."

"What has the house committee to do with it?"

"What do you mean what? They meet me and they ask: and when, my dear sir, will you register?"

"Oh, Lord," Philip Philippovich exclaimed despondently. "They meet, they ask . . . I can imagine what you tell them. You know I forbade you to hang around the stairways."

"What am I, a convict?" the man was astonished, and his sense of righteousness lit up even in his ruby. "What do you mean, 'hanging around'? Those are pretty insulting words, they are. I walk, like everybody else."

And he rubbed his patent feet against each other on the parquet.

Philip Philippovich was silent and looked away. After all, I must control myself, he thought. He went to the sideboard and emptied a glass of water in one breath.

"Very well," he spoke more calmly. "We're not discussing words now. And what does your charming house committee say?"

"What can it say. . . . And you don't have to call it names—'charming!' It defends the interests."

"Whose interests, if I may inquire?"

"Whose! Naturally—the interests of the working class."

Philip Philippovich's eye bulged.

"And what makes you a worker?"

"Well, naturally—I'm no bourgeois, no NEP-man."

"All right. Fine. And what does it want in defense of your revolutionary interests?"

"What does it want! It wants to register me. They say—who ever saw such a thing, for a man to live in Moscow unregistered? That's one. But the main thing is the registration card. I don't wish to be a deserter. And then—the trade union, the labor exchange. . . ."

"Would you mind telling me, how am I to register you? By what documents? My passport? Or this table-cloth? After all, the situation must be taken into account. Don't forget that you are . . . z . . . hm. . . . After all, you are, so to speak, an unexpectedly evolved being, a . . . a laboratory product." Philip Philippovich spoke less and less confidently.

The man remained triumphantly silent.

"Fine. But tell me, finally, what must be done to register you and, generally, to arrange matters according to your house committee's requirements? After all, you have no name, and no surname."

"There you're wrong. I can perfectly well choose a name. Have it printed in the newspaper, and that's that."

"And what do you wish to call yourself?"

The man adjusted his tie and answered:

"Polygraph Polygraphovich."

"Stop playing the fool," Philip Philippovich said glumly. "I am talking seriously to you."

A caustic grin twisted the man's seedy little mustache.

"I can't seem to understand it," he said gaily and reasonably. "I'm forbidden to swear. I'm forbidden to spit. But all I hear from you is 'fool' and 'fool.' I guess only professors are allowed to use insulting words in the Ar-es-ef-es-ar."

The blood rushed to Philip Philippovich's head. He tried to fill his glass with water, but dropped it, and it broke. Taking a drink from another glass, he thought to himself: A little more, and he'll start lecturing me, and he'll be entirely right. I don't keep a grip on myself.

He returned, bowed with exaggerated courtesy, and said with iron firmness:

"For-give me. My nerves are shot. Your name seemed rather odd to me. Where did you dig it up, I would be interested to know?"

"The house committee helped me. We looked through a calendar. They asked which name I liked, and I picked that one."

"There can be no such name in any calendar."

"It's really surprising," the man said with a smirk, "when there's one hanging in your own examination room."

Without getting up, Philip Philippovich leaned back in his chair to the button on the wall, and Zina appeared.

"Get me the calendar from the examination room."

There was a pause. When Zina returned with the calendar, Philip Philippovich asked:

"Where?"

"March 4th."

"Show me . . . Hm . . . I'll be. . . . Throw it in the stove, Zina, immediately."

Zina, her eyes bulging with fright, hurried out with the calendar, and the man shook his head deploringly.

"And may I know the surname?"

"The surname can be hereditary, that's all right with me."

"Hereditary? Meaning what?"
"Sharikov."

Before the desk in the office stood the chairman of
the house committee in a leather jacket. Dr. Bormenthal sat in an armchair. The doctor's face, glowing
from the frost (he had just returned), looked as helplessly bewildered as the face of Philip Philippovich,
who sat next to him.

"What shall I write?" he asked impatiently.

"Oh, well," said Shvonder. "It's a simple business.
Write out a certificate, citizen Professor. Certifying
such and such, you know, and that the bearer of same
is in fact Polygraph Polygraphovich Sharikov, hm . . .
originating, you know . . . from your apartment."

Bormenthal stirred in his chair with a look of per-
plexity. Philip Philippovich twitched his mustache.

"Hm . . . what a predicament! I couldn't imagine
anything more stupid. Originating! He didn't orig-
inate, but simply . . . well, in a word. . . ."

"That's your business," Shvonder said with calm
malice, "whether he originated or not. . . . When all
is said and done, Professor, it was your experiment!
It was you who created citizen Sharik."

"It's perfectly simple," Sharikov barked from his
place near the bookcase. He was peering at his tie, reflected in the depths of the glass.

"I would be very grateful," Philip Philippovich
snapped back, "if you kept out of the conversation. It
isn't 'perfectly simple.' It isn't simple at all."

"Why should I keep out?" Sharikov mumbled in an
offended tone, and Shvonder immediately came to his
support.

"Excuse me, Professor, but citizen Sharikov is entirely right. It is certainly his right to participate in
the discussion of his own fate, especially insofar as it

has to do with documents. A document is the most important thing in the world."

An earsplitting clangor interrupted the conversation. Philip Philippovich said into the receiver, "Yes. . . ." Then he turned red and shouted:

"I'll ask you not to disturb me with trifles. What business is it of yours?" And he slammed down the receiver.

Heavenly joy spread over Shvonder's face.

Turning purple, Philip Philippovich shouted:

"Make it short, let's get it over with."

He tore a sheet from his note pad and scribbled several words, then he read them aloud with irritation:

"'This will certify . . .' The devil take it . . . Hm . . . 'The bearer of this, a man produced in a laboratory experiment by means of a brain operation, requires documents . . .' damn it! I'm against getting those idiotic documents, anyway. 'Signed, Professor Preobrazhensky.'"

Shvonder took offense. "It's rather strange, Professor, how can you call documents idiotic? I cannot permit the presence of a documentless tenant in the house, especially when he isn't on the militia's military rolls. What if a war breaks out with the imperialist sharks?"

"I won't go to no wars!" Sharikov yipped suddenly into the bookcase.

Shvonder was taken aback, but he quickly rallied and civilly remarked to Sharikov:

"Citizen Sharikov, your words are highly lacking in social consciousness. It is most essential to be registered in the military rolls."

"I'll register, but if it comes to fighting, they can kiss. . . ." Sharikov answered coldly, adjusting his bow.

It was Shvonder's turn to be embarrassed. Preobrazhensky threw a vexed and wretched glance at

Bormenthal, as if to say, "How is that for morality!"
Bormenthal replied with a meaningful nod.

"I was severely wounded during the operation,"
Sharikov whined morosely. "Look what they did to
me." And he pointed at his head. The fresh scar of the
operation stretched across his forehead.

"Are you an anarchist individualist?" asked Shvonder, his eyebrows raised high.

"I should have a white card," Sharikov answered.

"All right, that's not important right now," answered the surprised Shvonder. "The fact is that we'll
send the professor's note to the militia, and we'll get
a document."

"Look here, hm . . ." Philip Philippovich interrupted
him suddenly, apparently tormented by some thought.
"Do you happen to have a vacant room in the house?
I am willing to buy it."

Yellow sparks flickered in Shvonder's little brown
eyes.

"No, Professor, to my deepest regret. And nothing
is foreseen, either."

Philip Philippovich pursed his lips and was silent.
The telephone went off again like a maniac. Without
asking anything, Philip Philippovich threw the receiver off the hook, and, after spinning for a while in
the air, it remained suspended on its blue cord. Everyone gave a start. "The old man's nerves are shot,"
thought Bormenthal, and Shvonder, his eyes flashing,
bowed and went out.

Sharikov followed him, his shoes squeaking as he
walked.

The professor remained alone with Bormenthal.
After a silence, Philip Philippovich shook his head
rapidly and said:

"It's a nightmare, I swear. Did you see? Do you
know, my dear doctor, these last two weeks have

worn me out more than the previous fourteen years. What a character, I'll tell you! . . ."

There was a muffled sound of cracking glass in the distance, followed by a woman's shriek, which rose and broke off. Some strange unholy power brushed against the wallpaper outside, in the direction of the examination room; there it threw something down with a crash, and instantly flew back. Doors banged, and Darya Petrovna's low cry came from the kitchen. Then Sharikov howled.

"Good Lord, what now!" cried Philip Philippovich, rushing to the door.

"A cat," Bormenthal guessed and ran out after him. They dashed down the corridor to the foyer, burst in, and turned into the hallway leading to the bathroom. Zina dashed out from the kitchen door and collided with Philip Philippovich.

"How many times did I say—no cats!" Philip Philippovich shouted in a rage. "Where is he? Ivan Arnoldovich, for God's sake, calm down the patients in the waiting room!"

"In the bathroom, the devil, he's in the bathroom," Zina cried, gasping. Philip Philippovich threw himself against the bathroom door, but it would not give.

"Open up this very second!"

In answer, something jumped against the walls of the locked bathroom, basins came clattering down, and Sharikov's wild voice roared hoarsely behind the door: "I'll kill you on the spot. . . ."

Water rushed down the pipes and began to run. Philip Philippovich pushed the door, trying to force it open. Darya Petrovna, flushed from the stove, appeared on the kitchen threshold, her face distorted. Then the transom window, high up on the wall between the bathroom and the kitchen, cracked jaggedly. Two pieces of glass crashed down, followed by an enormous tom with tiger stripes and a pale-blue bow on his neck, looking for all the world like an old-style policeman. He dropped right into a long platter on the table, splitting it in half, bounced off to the floor, turned around on three paws, waved the right paw as in a dance, and immediately seeped out through a narrow crack to the backstairs. The crack widened, and the tom was replaced by an old woman's face in a kerchief. Her skirt, flickering with white polka dots, moved into the kitchen. The old woman wiped her sunken mouth with her thumb and forefinger, ran her swollen, prickly little eyes around the kitchen, and said in a voice burning with curiosity:

"Oh, Heavenly Father!"

The pale Philip Philippovich crossed the kitchen and asked her menacingly:

"What do you want?"

"Just a little peek at the talking dog," the crone wheedled and crossed herself. Philip Philippovich blanched still more, walked up to the old woman and whispered, choking: "Out of the kitchen, this minute, out!"

The crone backed away toward the door and said resentfully:

"Don't have to be so high and mighty about it, Mr. Professor."

"Out, I say!" Philip Philippovich repeated and his eyes became as round as the owl's. He slammed the back door after her himself. "Darya Petrovna, I've asked you before."

"Philip Philippovich," Darya Petrovna cried despairingly, clenching her raised fists, "what am I to do? People are barging in all day. Sometimes I feel like dropping everything. . . ."

The water in the bathroom roared with muffled menace, but the voice could no longer be heard. Dr. Bormenthal came in.

"Ivan Arnoldovich, I beg you . . . hm . . . how many patients are waiting out there?"

"Eleven," said Bormenthal.

"Send them all away, I won't see anyone today."

Philip Philippovich knocked on the door with his knuckles and shouted:

"Come out this very minute! Why did you lock the door?"

"Boo-hoo!" Sharikov's muted voice replied piteously.

"What the devil! . . . I can't hear you, shut off the water."

"Bow! Wow!"

"Shut off the water, I say! What did he do there, I can't understand . . . ." Philip Philippovich shouted, flying into a frenzy. Zina and Darya opened the kitchen door and peeked out. Philip Philippovich banged his fist on the door again.

"There he is!" cried Darya Petrovna from the kitchen. Philip Philippovich rushed there. The physiognomy of Polygraph Polygraphovich appeared in the broken transom under the ceiling and thrust itself into the kitchen. It was twisted, the eyes were weepy, and a fresh, bloody scratch flamed along his nose.

"Have you gone crazy?" Philip Philippovich asked. "Why don't you come out?"

Sharikov looked around with fear and anguish:

"I locked myself in."

"Open the lock. Haven't you ever seen a lock?"

"The damned thing won't turn!" cried the frightened Polygraph.

"Heavens! He locked the safety catch!" Zina exclaimed, clapping her hands.

"There's a little button there!" Philip Philippovich shouted, trying to be heard above the water. "Press it down . . . Down! Press down!"

Sharikov disappeared, and reappeared a moment later in the transom.

"Can't see a thing in this bitchy dark," he howled, into the window, terrified.

"Turn on the light. He's gone mad!"

"The damned tom smashed the bulb," said Sharikov. "I tried to catch the bastard by the legs and the faucet came off. I can't find it now."

All three clapped their hands and remained frozen in this position.

Five minutes later Bormenthal, Zina, and Darya Petrovna sat side by side on the wet rug, rolled up at the foot of the door, and pressed it with their rear ends to the crack under the door, while the doorman Fyodor, with Darya Petrovna's lighted wedding candle in his hand, climbed up a wooden ladder and squeezed himself through the transom. His rear, dressed in large gray checks, flashed in the air and disappeared in the opening.

"Doo. . . woo-goo!" Sharikov was yelling something through the roar of the water.

Then Fyodor's voice was heard:

"Philip Philippovich, we have to open anyway, let it spread, we'll pump it out in the kitchen."

"Open!" Philip Philippovich cried angrily.

The three rose from the rug, pressed the bathroom door, and a flood of water streamed into the hallway. There it divided into three currents: one went directly opposite into the toilet, the other, right, into the kitchen, and the third, left, into the foyer. Splashing and jumping, Zina shut the door into the foyer. Fyodor came out, ankle-deep in water, smiling for some reason. He was all wet, as though dressed in oilcloth.

"Just barely stuffed it, the pressure's so high," he explained.

"Where is he?" asked Philip Philippovich, raising one foot and swearing.

"He's afraid to come out," Fyodor explained with a foolish grin.

"Will you hit me, dad?" Sharikov's plaintive voice came from the bathroom.

"Moron!" Philip Philippovich answered shortly.

Zina and Darya Petrovna, bare-legged, their skirts tucked up above their knees, and Sharikov with the doorman, with bare feet and rolled up trousers, dragged wet rags over the kitchen floor and squeezed them out into dirty pails and the sink. The neglected stove hummed. The water streamed out under the door onto the echoing stairway and fell down the stairwell into the cellar.

Bormenthal stood on his toes in a deep puddle in the foyer and spoke through the slightly opened door, held by the chain.

"There will be no visiting hours today, the professor is ill. Be so kind to step away from the door, we have a burst pipe..."

"But when will he receive?" insisted the voice behind the door. "I want to see him for just a moment...."

"Impossible," Bormenthal shifted from his toes to his heels. "The professor is in bed, and the pipe burst. Come back tomorrow, please. Zina! My dear! Wipe it up here, or it will pour out on the front stairs."

"The rags won't soak it up."

"We'll scoop it out with cups in a minute," said Fyodor, "in just a minute."

The bell rang continuously, and Bormenthal now stood on his soles in the water.

"But when will the operation take place?" a voice

persisted and tried to push into the crack.

"Our pipe burst . . ."

"I'm wearing overshoes. . ."

Bluish silhouettes appeared behind the door.

"Impossible, tomorrow, please."

"I have an appointment."

"Tomorrow. We've had an accident with the plumbing."

Fyodor crawled about at his feet in the pool, scraped with his tin cup, and the scratched Sharikov devised a new method. He rolled up a huge rag into a tube, lay down on his stomach in the water, and drove it from the foyer back toward the toilet.

"Damned goblin, stop driving it all over the apartment!" Darya Petrovna cried angrily. "Pour it into the sink."

"To hell with the sink," Sharikov replied, catching the muddy water with his hands, "it's starting to come out on the front stairs."

A bench rode in, screeching, from the hallway, with Philip Philippovich in blue striped socks stretched out, balancing himself on it.

"Ivan Arnoldovich, quit answering. Come to the bedroom, I will give you slippers."

"It's all right, Philip Philippovich, it doesn't matter."

"Put on galoshes."

"It doesn't matter. My feet are wet, anyway."

"Oh, God," Philip Philippovich moaned.

"What a vile beast!" Sharikov spoke up suddenly and slithered out, squatting on his haunches, with a soup bowl in his hand.

Bormenthal slammed the door. He could not restrain himself any longer, and burst out laughing. Philip Philippovich's nostrils flared and his glasses glinted.

"To whom are you referring," he asked Sharikov from his height, "if I may know?"

"The tom, of course. Such scum," replied Sharikov, his eyes shifting from corner to corner.

"You know, Sharikov," Philip Philippovich said, catching his breath, "I have positively never seen a more brazen creature than you."

Bormenthal snickered.

"You are simply an impudent wretch. How dare you say that? You've wreaked all this havoc, and you permit yourself . . . No! It's a damned outrage!"

"Sharikov, will you please tell me," Bormenthal put in, "how long you will go on chasing cats? Shame on you! It's disgraceful! You're a savage!"

"What sort of savage am I," Sharikov answered glumly. "I ain't no savage. It's impossible to stand him in the house. All he does is look around for something to filch. He gobbled up Darya's stuffing. I wanted to teach him a lesson."

"You need to be taught a lesson yourself," said Philip Philippovich. "Take a look at yourself in the mirror."

"He almost scratched my eye out," Sharikov responded, scowling, and put up a dirty hand to his eye.

By the time the darkened, water-logged parquet dried out a little, all the mirrors were covered with a steamy film and the bell had ceased ringing. Philip Philippovich stood in the foyer in red morocco slippers.

"Here, Fyodor, that's for you."

"Thank you kindly."

"Change immediately. And wait—have a drink first, Darya Petrovna will give you some vodka."

"Thank you kindly," Fyodor hesitated a little, then said, "There's something else, Philip Philippovich. I am sorry, it's really an embarrassment. But there's the glass in Apartment 7. Citizen Sharikov threw stones . . ."

"At a cat?" asked Philip Philippovich, turning dark as a cloud.

"That's the point—at the master of the apartment.

He's threatened to sue already."

"The devil!"

"Sharikov put his arms around their cook, and he told him to get out. So they had a squabble."

"For heaven's sake, you must always report such things to me immediately! . . . How much?"

"One and a half."

Philip Philippovich took three shiny coins from his pocket and handed them to Fyodor.

"A ruble and a half for such a scoundrel," a hollow voice came from the doorway. "Why, he himself . . ."

Philip Philippovich spun around, bit his lip, silently pushed Sharikov into the waiting room and locked the door. Sharikov immediately began to hammer on the door with his fists.

"Don't you dare!" Philip Philippovich exclaimed in the voice of a man who was obviously sick.

"Well, really," Fyodor remarked significantly. "I've never seen such nerve in my life."

Bormenthal appeared as from under the earth.

"Philip Philippovich, I beg you, calm down."

The energetic doctor unlocked the door to the waiting room and his voice was heard saying: "Where do you think you are? In a tavern?"

"That's right," Fyodor approved with emphasis, "that's right . . . He ought to land him one on the ear too . . ."

"Oh, what are you saying, Fyodor," Philip Philippovich mumbled sadly.

"It's you I'm sorry for, Philip Philippovich."

VII

"No, no, and no!" Bormenthal said insistently. "Be so good as to tuck it in."

"Oh, for God's sake," grumbled Sharikov.

"Thank you, Doctor," Philip Philippovich said warmly, "I'm tired of reprimanding him."

"I will not let you eat until you tuck it in. Zina, take away his plate."

"What do you mean, 'take away'?" Sharikov protested unhappily. "I'll put it on right away."

With his left hand he shielded the plate from Zina, and with the right he stuffed the napkin into his collar, which made him look like a customer in a barbershop.

"And use a fork, please," added Bormenthal.

With a deep sigh, Sharikov began to fish for pieces of sturgeon in the thick sauce.

"Another shot of vodka?" he said tentatively.

"Don't you think you've had enough?" asked Bormenthal. "You've been overdoing it lately."

"D'you stint me?" inquired Sharikov with a sullen look.

"You're talking nonsense . . . ." Philip Philippovich broke in sternly, but Bormenthal interrupted him.

"Don't worry, Philip Philippovich, I'll manage. You are talking rubbish, Sharikov, and the most outrageous thing is that you're so categorical and positive about it.

Of course, I don't stint you, particularly since the vodka isn't mine, but Philip Philippovich's. Simply, it's unhealthy. That is one reason. And the other is that you behave indecently even without vodka."

Bormenthal pointed to the taped-over sideboard.

"Zinusha, may I have more fish, please?" said the professor.

Sharikov, meantime, stretched his hand toward the carafe and, with a sidelong glance at Bormenthal, poured himself a glassful.

"And you must offer it to others, too," said Bormenthal. "First you serve Philip Philippovich, then me, and, last, yourself."

A faint, sarcastic smile touched Sharikov's lips as he poured the vodka into the glasses.

"All those rules you keep to, always on parade," he said. "Napkin here, tie there, and 'pardon me,' and 'please,' and 'merci'—but for the real thing, it isn't there. Torturing your own selves, just like in Tsarist times."

"And what would 'the real thing' be, if one may ask?"

Sharikov did not answer Philip Philippovich. Instead, he raised his glass and said:

"Well, here's to you . . ."

"And you, too," Bormenthal replied with some irony.

Sharikov poured the contents of the glass down his throat, screwed up his face, brought a piece of bread to his nose, sniffed it, then swallowed it, and his eyes filled with tears.

"Long experience," Philip Philippovich said curtly and almost absently.

Bormenthal gave him a surprised, sidelong look.

"Pardon me . . ."

"Long experience!" Philip Philippovich repeated with a bitter shake of the head. "Nothing to be done here—Klim."

Bormenthal peered sharply into his eyes and asked with lively interest:

"Do you think so, Philip Philippovich?"

"Think? I am certain."

"Can it really . . ." Bormenthal began and stopped, glancing at Sharikov, who frowned suspiciously.

"*Spater . . .*" said Philip Philippovich in an undertone.

"*Gut,*" replied the assistant.

Zina brought in the turkey. Bormenthal poured Philip Philippovich red wine and offered it to Sharikov.

"Not for me. I'll stick to the vodka." His face became shiny, sweat stood out on his forehead, he began to feel jolly. Philip Philippovich was also mellowed by the drinks. His eyes cleared up, and he looked more benevolently at Sharikov, whose black head gleamed in the napkin like a fly in cream.

Bormenthal, on the other hand, was stimulated to activity.

"Well, and what shall we do this evening?" he asked Sharikov.

The latter blinked and said:

"The circus, I think, best of all."

"Every day the circus," Philip Philippovich remarked benignly. "It's pretty boring, to my mind. In your place, I would go to the theater for once."

"I won't go to the theater," Sharikov said peevishly and made a sign of the cross over his mouth.

"Hiccuping at the table spoils other people's appetite," Bormenthal commented mechanically. "If you excuse me . . . Why don't you like the theater?"

Sharikov looked through the empty glass as through binoculars, pondered a while, and thrust out his lips.

"Nothing but fooling around . . . Talk, talk . . . Counterrevolution, that's what it is."

Philip Philippovich threw himself against the gothic

back of the chair and roared with laughter, so that his teeth glittered like a golden picket fence. Bormenthal only shook his head.

"Why don't you read something," he suggested. "Otherwise, you know . . ."

"Eh, I read and read . . ." answered Sharikov and with a quick, greedy movement poured himself half a glass of vodka.

"Zina," Philip Philippovich cried anxiously. "Take away the vodka, dear. We don't need it any more. And what do you read?"

A picture suddenly flashed through his mind: an uninhabited island, a palm tree, a man in an animal skin and cap. "I'll have to get him *Robinson* . . ."

"Oh, that . . . What d'you call it . . . the correspondence of Engels with that . . . what the devil's his name —Kautsky."

Bormenthal's hand with a piece of white meat on a fork stopped midway, and Philip Philippovich spilled his wine. Sharikov expertly downed the vodka.

Philip Philippovich put his elbows on the table, peered closely at Sharikov, and asked:

"And what is your opinion of it, if I may ask?"

Sharikov shrugged.

"I don't agree."

"With whom? With Engels, or with Kautsky?"

"With neither," answered Sharikov.

"That's marvelous, I swear. Everyone who says the other . . . And what would you propose yourself?"

"What's there to propose? . . . They write and write . . . congress, Germans . . . who knows them. . . Makes your head spin. Just take everything and divide it up . . ."

"I thought so," exclaimed Philip Philippovich, slamming his hand on the tablecloth. "Exactly what I thought."

"Do you know how to do it, too?" asked Bormenthal with curiosity.

"How, how," Sharikov began, growing voluble after the vodka. "It's plain enough. What do you think? One man spreads himself out in seven rooms and has forty pair of pants, and another hangs around garbage dumps, looking for something to eat."

"With regard to the seven rooms," Philip Philippovich inquired, narrowing his eyes with pride, "you are hinting at me, of course?"

Sharikov hunched his shoulders and said nothing.

"Very well, I am not against division. Doctor, how many patients did you send away yesterday?"

"Thirty-nine," Bormenthal replied instantly.

"Hm . . . three hundred ninety rubles. Well, let's divide the loss among the three men. We won't count the ladies—Zina and Darya Petrovna. Your share is one hundred thirty rubles, Sharikov. Kindly pay up."

"A fine thing," Sharikov became alarmed. "What's this for?"

"For the faucet, and for the cat," Philip Philippovich roared suddenly, losing his ironic calm.

"Philip Philippovich," Bormenthal cried anxiously.

"Wait. For the havoc you wreaked, which made it impossible for me to see my patients. It's intolerable. A man jumps around the whole house like a Neanderthal, breaks faucets. Who killed Mme. Polasikher's cat? Who . . ."

"And the other day, Sharikov, you bit a lady on the stairs," Bormenthal hastened to add.

"You are . . ." growled Philip Philippovich.

"She banged me on the jaw," squealed Sharikov. "It's my jaw, not the government's!"

"Because you pinched her breast," shouted Bormenthal, turning over a wine glass. "You are . . ."

"You are on the lowest rung of development," Philip

Philippovich shouted still more loudly. "You are a creature just in the process of formation, with a feeble intellect. All your actions are the actions of an animal. Yet you permit yourself to speak with utterly insufferable impudence in the presence of two people with a university education—to offer advice on a cosmic scale and of equally cosmic stupidity on how to divide everything . . . And right after gobbling up a boxful of toothpowder too . . ."

"The day before yesterday," confirmed Bormenthal.

"There!" thundered Philip Philippovich. "Just get it straight! Keep your nose out of things—and, incidentally, why did you rub off the zinc ointment from it?—and remember that you must keep quiet and listen to what you are told. Try to learn, try to become a more or less acceptable member of socialist society. And, by the way, what scoundrel supplied you with that book?"

"Everybody's a scoundrel to you," said the frightened Sharikov, overwhelmed by the two-sided attack.

"I can guess," Philip Philippovich exclaimed, flushing angrily.

"Well, so what? So Shvonder gave it to me. He is no scoundrel . . . To help me develop . . ."

"I see how you are developing after Kautsky," Philip Philippovich screamed in a falsetto, his face turning yellow. He furiously pressed the button in the wall. "Today's case demonstrates it perfectly. Zina!"

"Zina!" cried Bormenthal.

"Zina!" howled the terrified Sharikov.

Zina came running. She was pale.

"Zina, out there in the waiting room . . . It is in the waiting room?"

"It is," Sharikov answered submissively. "Green, like vitriol."

"A green book . . ."

"Now they'll burn it," Sharikov cried desperately. "It belongs to the government, it's from the library."

"It's called *Correspondence*—between what's his name, Engels, and that devil . . . Into the stove with it!"

Zina flew out.

"I'd hang that Shvonder, I swear I would, on the first dry branch," cried Philip Philippovich, furiously driving his fork into a turkey wing. "The astonishing swine, like an abscess on the house. It's not enough for him to write all sorts of senseless libels in the newspapers . . ."

Sharikov began to squint at the professor with ironic malice. Philip Philippovich, in turn, sent him a sidelong glance and broke off.

Oh, things won't come to any good in this apartment, I'm afraid, Bormenthal suddenly thought prophetically.

Zina brought in a round tray with a coffee pot and a rum cake, yellow on one side and browned on the other.

"I won't eat it," Sharikov declared at once with a threatening air.

"No one asks you to. Just behave decently. Doctor, please."

The dinner ended in silence.

Sharikov pulled a crumpled cigarette from his pocket and began to smoke. After the coffee, Philip Philippovich looked at his watch, pressed the repeater, and it delicately chimed eight-fifteen. Philip Philippovich leaned against the gothic chair back, as his custom was, and reached for the newspaper on the small table.

"Doctor, would you please take him to the circus? But, for God's sake, take a look at the program first —make sure they have no cats."

"How do they let such trash into the circus?" Sharikov wondered morosely, shaking his head.

"They let in all sorts," Philip Philippovich responded ambiguously. "What do they have?"

"In Solomonsky's Circus," Bormenthal began to read, "there are four . . . Yuesems, whatever they are, and a man at dead center."

"What sort of Yuesems?" Philip Philippovich inquired suspiciously.

"Heaven knows. First time I've seen the word."

"Well, then you'd better see what's at Nikitin's. We must make sure."

"At Nikitin's . . . At Nikitin's . . . hm . . . 'elephants, and the ultimate in human agility.'"

"I see. What will you say to elephants, my dear Sharikov?" Philip Philippovich asked Sharikov doubtfully. The latter was offended.

"What do you think, I don't understand anything? A cat is something else. Elephants are useful animals," he answered.

"Very well, excellent. If they are useful, go and take a look at them. And listen to Ivan Arnoldovich. No conversations in the buffet! Ivan Arnoldovich, I beg you, don't give Sharikov any beer."

Ten minutes later, Ivan Arnoldovich and Sharikov, in a cap with a duckbill visor and a heavy coat with the collar turned up, went off to the circus. The apartment was quiet. Philip Philippovich went into his office and turned on the lamp with the thick green shade. The huge room was peaceful in the muted light, and he began to pace back and forth. The tip of his cigar glowed for a long time with a pale-green fire. The professor walked with his hands in his trouser pockets, and some persistent thought seemed to torment the learned brow under the thinning hair. He smacked his lips, hummed "toward the sacred banks of the Nile" through his teeth, and muttered something. Finally, he put down the cigar in an ash tray, went to the cabinet made entirely of glass, and turned on the three powerful ceiling lights, illuminating the whole office. From the third shelf in the cabinet, Philip Philippovich took out a narrow jar and began to study it, frowning, against the light. In the transparent, heavy liquid, the small white lump extracted from the depths of Sharik's brain was floating, without dropping to the bottom. Shrugging his shoulders, twisting his lips and grunting, Philip Philippovich devoured it with his eyes, as though trying to find in the white floating lump the reasons for the remarkable events that had turned all life in the Prechistenka apartment topsy-turvy.

It is very possible that the learned gentleman discovered those reasons. In any event, having stared his fill at the hypophysis, he returned the jar to the cabinet, locked it, and put the key in his vest pocket. After that, he threw himself onto the leather sofa, his head drawn into his shoulders and his hands deep in the pockets of his jacket. For a long time he burned a second cigar, chewing its end to a pulp, and finally, in total solitude, green, looking like an aged Faust, he exclaimed:

"By God, I think I will."

No one answered him. All sounds had died out in the apartment. By eleven, as we know, all traffic stops in Obukhov Lane. Infrequently, the steps of a belated pedestrian were heard in the distance, tapping somewhere beyond the curtains and dying away. The repeater in Philip Philippovich's pocket tinkled delicately under his fingers. . . . The professor impatiently awaited the return of Dr. Bormenthal and Sharikov from the circus.

VIII

No one knows what decision Philip Philippovich had come to that night. He undertook nothing unusual in the course of the following week, and it was, perhaps, because of his inaction that life in the apartment was overwhelmed with events.

About six days after the incident of the tom and the water, a young man representing the house committee came to see Sharikov. The young man, who turned out to be a woman, handed Sharikov his documents, which he immediately stuffed into his pocket. Directly after that he called Dr. Bormenthal.

"Bormenthal!"

"Be kind enough to address me by name and patronymic!" Bormenthal answered, changing in the face. It must be said that in the course of those six days the surgeon had managed to have some eight quarrels with his charge, and the atmosphere in the apartment in Obukhov Lane was torrid.

"Well, then, call me by name and patronymic too!" Sharikov replied with complete justice.

"No!" Philip Philippovich thundered in the doorway. "I will not permit such a name and patronymic to be pronounced in my home. If you want us to stop addressing you familiarly as Sharikov, both Dr. Bormenthal and I will call you 'Mr. Sharikov.'"

"I am not a mister, all the misters are in Paris!" barked Sharikov.

"Shvonder's work!" shouted Philip Philippovich. "Very well, I shall settle accounts with that rascal. While I am in my home, there will be no one here but misters! Otherwise, either you or I shall leave, and it is most likely to be you. Today I shall place an ad in the newspapers, and I shall find you a room."

"So, you think I'm fool enough to leave this place?" Sharikov replied with utmost emphasis.

"What?" asked Philip Philippovich, and changed color so violently that Bormenthal rushed up to him and took him by the sleeve with anxious tenderness.

"You know, you had better stop your insolence, Monsieur Sharikov!" Bormenthal raised his voice. Sharikov stepped back, took three slips of paper from his pocket—one green, one yellow, and one white—and, poking his finger at them, said:

"Here. Member of the tenants' association. Assigned an area of sixteen square *arshin.** And it says definitely: Apartment Number 5; responsible lessee, Preobrazhensky." Sharikov thought a moment, and added a phrase which Bormenthal automatically noted in his mind as new: "If you please."

Philip Philippovich bit his lip and, forgetting all caution, hissed out through it:

"I swear, I will shoot this Shvonder in the end."

Sharikov listened to these words with the keenest attention, as evidenced by his eyes.

"Philip Philippovich, *forsichtig* . . ." Bormenthal warned.

"Well, you know . . . If it's a question of such baseness! . . ." Philip Philippovich exclaimed in Russian. "But bear it in mind, Sharikov . . . Mister, that I . . .

---

* Approximately twelve square yards.

that if you permit yourself just one more insolent outburst, you shall get no more dinners or any other meals in my home. Sixteen *arshin* are delightful, but that frog-green paper of yours does not oblige me to feed you!"

Sharikov was alarmed and his jaw dropped.

"I can't go without eating," he muttered. "Where will I get my grub?"

"In that case, behave yourself!" both doctors declared in chorus.

Sharikov was subdued for the rest of the day and did no damage to anyone except himself. Taking advantage of Bormenthal's brief absence, he took possession of his razor and slashed his cheek so badly that Philip Philippovich and Dr. Bormenthal had to stitch the cut, which made Sharikov howl long and piteously, weeping bitter tears.

On the following night two men sat in the green dusk in the professor's office—Philip Philippovich himself, and his loyal and devoted assistant, Dr. Bormenthal. Everyone else in the apartment was asleep. Philip Philippovich was dressed in his azure robe and red slippers, and Bormenthal was in his shirt-sleeves and blue suspenders. On the round table between the doctors, next to the plump album, stood a bottle of cognac, a saucer with lemon, and a box of cigars. The scientists, who had filled the room with smoke, heatedly discussed the latest event. That evening Sharikov had appropriated two chervontsy, which he had found under the paperweight in Philip Philippovich's office, and disappeared, returning late at night, hopelessly drunk. But that was not all. He was accompanied by two unknown individuals who raised a row on the front stairs, demanding to spend the night in the apartment as Sharikov's guests. These individuals departed only after Fyodor, who had come upon the scene in a heavy coat over his underwear, telephoned the 45th precinct of the militia. They beat an instant retreat as soon as Fyodor hung up the receiver. Following their exit, the malachite ash tray was found to be mysteriously missing from the pier-glass table in the foyer, along with Philip Philippovich's beaver hat and his cane, on which there was an inscription in gold inlay: "To our beloved and esteemed Philip Philippovich from his grateful interns, on . . ." This was followed by the Roman numeral "X."

"Who are they?" Philip Philippovich bore down on Sharikov with clenched fists. Swaying and clinging to the coats, Sharikov muttered that he did not know them, but that they were not some trashy sons of bitches, but good men.

"The most astonishing thing is that both were drunk . . . How did they manage it?" Philip Philippovich exclaimed, staring with wonder at the stand which used to hold the memento of his anniversary.

"Specialists," explained Fyodor, going back to bed with a ruble in his pocket.

Sharikov flatly denied any knowledge of the two chervontsy, mumbling inarticulately that he was not the only one in the apartment.

"Ah, then, perhaps, it was Dr. Bormenthal who pinched them?" inquired Philip Philippovich in a low but terrifying voice.

Sharikov swayed, opened his utterly glassy eyes, and offered a hypothesis:

"Maybe Zinka took'em . . ."

"What? . . ." shrieked Zina, who appeared in the doorway like a ghost in an unbuttoned blouse, her hand over her breast. "How dare he? . . ."

Philip Philippovich's neck turned red.

"Calm down, Zinusha," he said, stretching a hand

toward her. "Don't get excited, we'll take care of everything."

Zina broke into sobs, her lips quivering loosely and her hand heaving up and down over her shoulder blade.

"Zina, aren't you ashamed? Would anyone suspect you? Such a disgrace!" Bormenthal spoke helplessly.

"Oh, Zina, what a fool you are, heaven forgive me," Philip Philippovich began.

But Zina's sobs had stopped of themselves, and everybody was silent. Sharikov began to feel sick. Knocking his head against the wall, he uttered a sound—something like "ee-ee" or "eh-h!" His face blanched and his jaws began to work convulsively.

"A pail, get a pail for the scoundrel! In the examination room!"

And everybody ran to take care of the sick Sharikov. Later, when he was being led off to bed, he swayed in Bormenthal's arms and swore tenderly and melodiously, his tongue twisting over the obscenities.

The entire incident occurred at about 1 o'clock, and now it was three in the morning, but the two in the office were wide awake, stimulated by the cognac and lemon. The smoke in the room was so thick that it floated in slow, dense, horizontal layers, without a quiver.

Dr. Bormenthal, pale, with resolute eyes, raised a glass with a stem as slender as a dragonfly.

"Philip Philippovich," he exclaimed in a voice full of emotion, "I shall never forget how I came to you as a half-starved student, and you gave me a place in the department. Believe me, Philip Philippovich, you are much more to me than a professor, a teacher . . . My immense regard for you . . . Permit me to kiss you, my dear Philip Philippovich."

"Surely, my dear friend . . ." Philip Philippovich

mumbled with embarrassment and rose toward him. Bormenthal embraced him and planted a kiss on his fluffy, smoke-browned mustache.

"Believe me, Philip Phili . . ."

"I am so moved, so moved . . . Thank you," spoke Philip Philippovich. "My dear, I shout at you sometimes during operations. Forgive an old man's temper. In fact, you know, I am so lonely . . . From Seville and to Granada . . ."

"Philip Philippovich, how can you? . . ." the fiery Bormenthal exclaimed with all sincerity. "Don't speak of such things to me again if you don't want to offend me . . . ."

"Well, thank you . . . Toward the sacred banks of the Nile . . . Thank you . . . And I have become very fond of you as a capable physician."

"Philip Philippovich, I say to you . . ." Bormenthal exclaimed passionately. He rushed to the door leading into the hallway, closed it more firmly, and returned, continuing in a whisper, "it is the only solution. Of course, I would not presume to advise you, but, Philip Philippovich, look at yourself, you are utterly worn out, it is impossible to go on working under such conditions!"

"Absolutely impossible," Philip Philippovich agreed, sighing.

"Well, you see, it's unthinkable," whispered Bormenthal. "Last time you said you were afraid for me, if you knew, my dear Professor, how you moved me by it. But I am not a boy, I realize myself how badly it might turn out. But I am deeply convinced there is no other way out."

Philip Philippovich got up, waved his hands and exclaimed:

"Don't tempt me, don't even mention it." The professor began to pace the room, and the layers of smoke billowed around him. "I won't listen. Do you understand what will happen if we're caught? We'll never get away with it, even if it is our first offense, particularly 'taking into account the social origin.' Your origin isn't too suitable, either, is it, my dear?"

"Suitable! My father was an examining magistrate in Vilno," Bormenthal replied dolefully, finishing his cognac.

"There you are. It's a rotten heredity. Couldn't imagine anything nastier. But no, excuse me, mine is even worse. My father was an archpriest in a cathedral. Merci. From Seville and to Granada . . . in the quiet of the night . . . the devil take it."

"Philip Philippovich, you are a world celebrity. They wouldn't . . . And for the sake, if you'll pardon the expression, of some son of a bitch. They wouldn't dare touch you!"

"That's all the more reason for not doing it," Philip Philippovich objected pensively, pausing to throw a glance at the glass cabinet.

"But why?"

"Because you are not a world celebrity."

"Oh, I . . ."

"There you are. As for abandoning a colleague in the event of a catastrophe, and getting off safely myself on the strength of my world reputation . . . Forgive me . . . I am a Moscow scientist, not Sharikov."

Philip Philippovich proudly lifted his shoulders and began to look like an old French king.

"Philip Philippovich, ah . . ." Bormenthal exclaimed ruefully. "But what else? Wait until we succeed in turning this hoodlum into a man?"

Philip Philippovich stopped him with a gesture of the hand, poured himself some cognac, sipped it, sucked on a slice of lemon, and began:

"Ivan Arnoldovich, what do you think, do I know

anything about the anatomy and physiology of, say, the human brain? What is your opinion?"

"Philip Philippovich, how can you ask!" Bormenthal answered with strong emotion, spreading his hands.

"Very well. False modesty aside, I also think I am not the least man in this field in Moscow."

"And I think that you are the first and greatest not only in Moscow, but also in London, and in Oxford!" Bormenthal broke in fervently.

"Oh, well, perhaps. And so, I say to you, future Professor Bormenthal—no one can ever succeed in that. Definitely not. You need not even ask. You may quote me. Say that Preobrazhensky said so. Finitas, Klim!" he suddenly proclaimed in solemn tones, and the instrument case replied with a delicate tinkle. "Klim," he repeated. "Bormenthal, you are my best pupil, and also my friend, as I have become convinced today. And I shall tell you in confidence, as a friend—and, of course, I know that you will not taunt me with it: the old ass Preobrazhensky pulled a boner with this operation like a third-year student. True, it led to a discovery, and you know what this discovery is yourself," Philip Philippovich dolefully pointed both hands at the window shade, evidently indicating Moscow. "But the only result of this discovery, Ivan Arnoldovich, will be that all of us will now have this Sharik up here," and Preobrazhensky patted himself on his thick, apoplectic neck. "You may rest assured! If anyone," Philip Philippovich went on voluptuously, "would stretch me out here and give me a whipping, I swear I would pay him five chervontsy! From Seville and to Granada... The devil take me . . . I spent five years digging out hypophyses from brains . . . Do you know what work went into it—the mind could not conceive! And now I ask you—what for? So that I might one day transform a perfectly delightful dog into such filthy scum that your hair stands up to think of it!"

"Something extraordinary!"

"Quite. And that's what happens, Doctor, when the investigator, instead of feeling his way and moving parallel to nature, forces the question and tries to raise the curtain: there, take your Sharikov and lump him."

"Philip Philippovich, but what if it were Spinoza's brain?"

"Yes!" barked Philip Philippovich. "Certainly! If the wretched mutt does not die under my knife—and you saw what kind of an operation this is. To put it briefly, I Philip Philippovich Preobrazhensky, have never done anything more difficult in my life. Certainly, it might be possible to graft the hypophysis of Spinoza or some such devil, and turn a dog into a highly advanced human. But what in hell for? Tell me, please, why is it necessary to manufacture Spinozas artificially when any peasant woman can produce them at any time? Didn't Mme. Lomonosov bear her famous offspring out in Kholmogory? Doctor, the human race takes care of this by itself, and every year, in the course of its evolution, it creates dozens of outstanding geniuses who adorn the earth, stubbornly selecting them out of the mass of scum. Do you understand now, Doctor, why I rejected your conclusions in Sharik's case history? My discovery, may it be damned, of which you make so much, isn't worth a rap . . . No, no, don't contradict me, Ivan Arnoldovich. I understand this now. You know I never throw words to the wind. Theoretically it is interesting, yes. The physiologists will be ecstatic. Moscow will go wild . . . But practically? Whom do we see before us?" Preobrazhensky pointed in the direction of the examination room, where Sharikov was taking his repose.

"An exceptional scoundrel."

"But who is he? Klim, Klim," cried the professor. "Klim Chugunkin (Bormenthal's mouth dropped open) —that's what it is: two arrests, alcoholism, 'divide everything,' my hat and two chervontsy gone (Philip Philippovich turned purple at the memory of his anniversary cane)—a boor and a swine . . . Never mind the cane, I will find it! In short, the hypophysis is a secret chamber which determines the aspect of the given human individual. The given one! From Seville and to Granada . . ." Philip Philippovich shouted, fiercely rolling his eyes, "and not the human aspect generally. It is the brain itself, in miniature. And I have no use for it, to the devil with it! I was concerned with something else altogether—eugenics, the improvement of the human species. And then I pull this boner with rejuvenation! You don't think I've been doing all those operations for the money? I am a scientist, after all."

"A great scientist!" said Bormenthal, swallowing some cognac. His eyes became bloodshot.

"I wanted to perform a little experiment, after I had first extracted the sex hormone from the hypophysis two years ago. And what did I get instead? Good Lord! These hormones in the hypophysis, oh, God . . . Doctor, I am before a hopeless dunce. I swear, I am utterly lost."

Bormenthal suddenly pushed up his sleeves and said, crossing his eyes to the tip of his nose:

"In that case, I will tell you, my dear teacher: if you don't want to do it, I shall give him arsenic at my own risk. To the devil with it, even if my father was an examining magistrate! After all, he is your own creature, the product of your experiment."

Philip Philippovich, suddenly extinguished, limp, sank deep into his chair.

"No, this I shall not permit, my dear boy. I am sixty years old, and I can advise you. Never attempt a crime, no matter against whom it might be directed. You must reach old age with clean hands."

"But, Philip Philippovich, what if that Shvonder goes on meddling with his 'education'? Good God, I am only just beginning to realize what this Sharikov can turn into!"

"Ah! It dawned on you? And I realized it ten days after the operation. But the point is that this Shvonder is the worst fool of all. He does not understand that Sharikov is a far greater menace to him than he is to me. Today he does everything to sick him on me, without realizing that if anyone should then turn him against Shvonder himself, nothing will be left of him or his."

"But of course! Look at that business with the cats! A man with the heart of a dog."

"Oh, no, no," Philip Philippovich sang out. "You are mistaken, Doctor. In heaven's name, don't malign the dog. The cats are only temporary . . . It's a question of discipline and two or three weeks. I assure you. Another month or so, and he will stop attacking them."

"But why not now?"

"Ivan Arnoldovich, that's elementary . . . Really, why are you asking? The hypophysis is not suspended in the air. After all, it was grafted onto a dog's brain. Give it time to take properly. Today Sharikov manifests only the remnants of a dog's nature, and you must realize that the cats are the least of his sins. The whole horror, you see, is that his heart is no longer a dog's heart, but a human one. And the vilest you could find!"

Bormenthal, beside himself, clenched his strong, lean hands into fists, moved his shoulders, and said firmly:

"Of course, I will kill him!"

"I forbid it!" Philip Philippovich replied emphatically.

"But . . ."

Philip Philippovich was suddenly alert and raised his finger.

"Wait . . . I thought I heard steps."

Both of them listened, but the hallway was quiet.

"It seemed to me," said Philip Philippovich, and began to speak heatedly in German. The Russian word "criminality" was heard several times in the flow of German phrases.

"One moment," Bormenthal suddenly said and stepped up to the door. The steps could now be heard clearly, approaching the office. Besides, a voice was mumbling something. Bormenthal flung open the door and sprang back with astonishment. The utterly stunned Phillip Philippovich remained frozen in his chair.

Before them, in the bright rectangle of the hallway, was Darya Petrovna, in nothing but a nightgown and with an angry, flaming face. Both the doctor and the professor were overwhelmed by the amplitude of her powerful and, as it seemed to them in the first moment of shock, entirely naked body. Darya Petrovna was dragging something behind her in her powerful hands, and this "something" resisted, trying to sit down on its rear and dragging its small feet, covered with black down, on the parquet. The "something" was, of course, Sharikov, utterly unnerved, still drunk, tousled, and wearing nothing but his undershirt.

Darya Petrovna, grandiose and naked, shook Sharikov like a sack of potatoes, and said:

"Look at him, Mr. Professor, look at our visitor Telegraph Telegraphovich. I was married, but Zina is an innocent girl. It's lucky I woke up."

Having delivered this tirade, Darya Petrovna suddenly realized her nakedness, covered her breast with her hands, and dashed away.

"Darya Petrovna, in heaven's name, excuse us," the

scarlet Philip Philippovich cried after her, recovering himself.

Bormenthal pushed up his shirt-sleeves still higher and made a move toward Sharikov. Philip Philippovich glanced into his eyes and was appalled. "Oh, no, Doctor! I forbid it . . ."

Bormenthal took Sharikov by the collar with his right hand and shook him so violently that the shirt ripped.

Philip Philippovich rushed to stop him and began to pull the puny Sharikov away from the surgeon's clutching hands.

"You have no right to hit me!" the half-choked Sharikov screamed, sitting down on the floor and sobering up.

"Doctor!" Philip Philippovich yelled.

Bormenthal collected himself a little and loosened his hold on Sharikov, upon which the latter immediately began to whimper.

"All right," hissed Bormenthal, "we'll wait till morning. I'll teach him a lesson when he sobers up." He seized Sharikov under the arms and dragged him off to the waiting room to sleep.

Sharikov made an attempt to kick, but his legs refused to obey him.

Philip Philippovich spread his feet wide, so that the azure skirts of his robe flared out, raised his hands and his eyes to the ceiling light in the hallway, and cried, "Well, well . . ."

IX

Sharikov's lesson, promised by Bormenthal, did not, however, take place on the following morning for the simple reason that Polygraph Polygraphovich had disappeared from home. Bormenthal flew into a frenzy of despair, called himself an ass for not hiding the front door key, shouted that it was unforgivable, and ended by wishing Sharikov to fall under a bus. Philip Philippovich sat in his office, his fingers in his hair, and said:

"I can imagine what will happen in the street. . . . I can i-ma-gine. From Seville and to Granada, good God . . ."

"He may still be at the house committee office," Bormenthal raged and ran off somewhere.

At the office he quarreled so violently with the house committee chairman, Shvonder, that the latter finally sat down to write a complaint to the people's court of the Khamovnichesky District. As he was writing the complaint, he shouted that it was not his duty to watch over Professor Preobrazhensky's ward, especially since Polygraph had only yesterday proved himself to be a crook, having taken seven rubles from the house committee, allegedly to buy textbooks at the cooperative store.

Fyodor earned three rubles by searching the house from top to bottom, but discovered no trace of Sharikov.

Only one fact was established: Polygraph had left at dawn in his cap, muffler and coat, with all his documents, a bottle of ashberry brandy from the sideboard, and Dr. Bormenthal's gloves. Darya Petrovna and Zina gave stormy vent to their jubilation and made no secret of their hope that Sharikov would never return. Darya Petrovna revealed that she had lent Sharikov three rubles and fifty kopeks only the day before.

"It serves you right!" growled Philip Philippovich, shaking his fists. The telephone rang all day and all of the following day. The doctors received an extraordinary number of patients. But on the third day they faced the question head on, and decided that the militia had to be notified so that it might search Sharikov out in the maelstrom of Moscow.

But no sooner had the word "militia" been spoken, than the reverential hush of Obukhov Lane was shattered by the barking of a truck, and the windows of the house shook. Then came a confident ring at the door, and Polygraph Polygraphovich made his appearance. He entered with an air of enormous dignity, removed his cap in total silence, hung up his coat on the horns of the coat rack, and presented himself in an entirely new state. He wore a leather jacket, obviously second-hand, frayed leather trousers, and high English boots, laced to the knee. An overpowering smell of cats immediately spread throughout the foyer. Preobrazhensky and Bormenthal crossed their arms on their chests as though by command, and took up positions at the doorway, awaiting the first words of Polygraph Polygraphovich. He smoothed his coarse hair, cleared his throat, and carefully studied himself in the mirror, obviously trying to mask his confusion by an air of utmost ease.

"Philip Philippovich," he finally began, "I have found myself a position."

Both doctors emitted an indefinite, dry, guttural

sound and stirred. Preobrazhensky recovered first. He held out his hand and said:

"Let me see the paper."

The document read: "This will certify that the bearer of same, Comrade Polygraph Polygraphovich Sharikov, is the director of the sub-section for purging the city of Moscow of stray animals (cats, etc.) of the Moscow Communal Property Administration."

"I see," Philip Philippovich said with difficulty. "And who arranged this for you? However, I can easily guess it myself."

"Well, yes, it was Shvonder," replied Sharikov.

"And may I inquire, what is this nauseating smell that you are spreading?"

Sharikov sniffed his jacket with a worried air.

"Well, what can you do, it smells . . . Naturally— it's the profession. We choked them and choked them yesterday . . . Cats."

Philip Philippovich gave a start and looked at Bormenthal. The doctor's eyes resembled two black muzzles of guns aimed straight at Sharikov. Without a word, he moved toward Sharikov and grabbed him easily and confidently by the throat.

"Help!" squealed Sharikov, turning pale.

"Doctor!"

"Don't worry, Philip Philippovich, I won't do anything wrong," Bormenthal replied in an iron voice and shouted: "Zina, Darya Petrovna!"

The women appeared in the foyer.

"Now repeat after me . . ." said Bormenthal, squeezing Sharikov's throat just a little as he leaned against the fur coat on the rack. "Forgive me . . ."

"Oh, all right, I'll repeat it," the utterly stunned Sharikov answered hoarsely. He suddenly filled his lungs with air, tried to break away and cry "Help," but the cry did not come out, and his head was pushed all the way into the fur.

"Doctor, I beg you."

Sharikov nodded his head, indicating that he submitted and would repeat the words.

". . . Forgive me, Darya Petrovna and Zinaida? . . ."

"Prokofievna," Zina said in a frightened whisper.

"Uph . . . Prokofievna . . . for permitting myself . . ."

"A filthy trick at night in a drunken state."

"Drunken . . ."

"I will never again . . ."

"Never ag . . ."

"Let him go, let him go, Ivan Arnoldovich," both women begged in chorus. "You'll strangle him."

Bormenthal released Sharikov and said:

"Is the truck waiting for you?"

"No," Polygraph replied respectfully, "it only brought me here."

"Zina, tell the driver he can go. Now listen here: have you come back to Philip Philippovich's apartment?"

"Where else am I to go?" Sharikov answered timidly, his eyes wandering.

"Fine. You'll behave now and watch your step. Any more trouble, and you'll have to deal with me. Is that clear?"

"It's clear," answered Sharikov.

Philip Philippovich remained silent throughout Sharikov's chastisement. He seemed to have shrunk pathetically as he stood by the door, chewing at his nail, eyes lowered to the parquet. Then he suddenly raised his eyes to Sharikov and asked in a flat, expressionless voice:

"And what do you do with those . . . with the cats you kill?"

"They'll be used for coats," said Sharikov. "They'll be made into squirrels and sold to workers on credit."

After that quiet reigned in the apartment. It lasted two days. Polygraph Polygraphovich left by truck, in the morning, returned in the evening, and dined quietly with Philip Philippovich and Bormenthal.

Although Bormenthal and Sharikov both slept in the waiting room, they did not speak to one another, and Bormenthal was the first to become restive.

Two days later a young lady appeared in the apartment. She was thin, with penciled eyebrows and cream-colored stockings, and she was visibly abashed at the magnificence of the apartment. Dressed in a shabby little coat, she followed Sharikov in and almost collided with the professor in the foyer.

The startled professor stopped short, screwed up his eyes, and asked:

"Explain, if you don't mind?"

"We're going to register. She is our typist, she'll live with me. Bormenthal will have to move from the waiting room. He has his own apartment," Sharikov said with gloomy animosity.

Philip Philippovich blinked several times, thought for a while, looking at the violently blushing young lady, and very civilly invited her in.

"Would you please step into my office for a moment?"

"I'll come with her," Sharikov said quickly and suspiciously.

At this point, Bormenthal materialized out of nowhere.

"Sorry," he said. "The professor will have a little chat with the lady, and we shall wait a while right here."

"I don't want to," Sharikov snapped back, trying to follow Philip Philippovich and the young lady, fiery with embarrassment.

"Now, if you'll excuse me," Bormenthal said, taking Sharikov by the wrist and leading him off into the examination room.

For some five minutes nothing was heard from the office, then suddenly there was the sound of muted sobs.

Philip Philippovich was standing near the table, and the young lady was crying into a soiled lace handkerchief.

"He said, the rotter, that he was wounded in the war," the young lady sobbed.

"He is lying," Philip Philippovich answered implacably. He shook his head and continued. "I am sincerely sorry for you, but this is impossible, my child ... One should not take up with just anyone, simply because of hs job ... Now look here ..." He opened the desk drawer and brought out three bills of three chervontsy each.

"I'll poison myself," the young lady cried. "Every day it's corned beef in the cafeteria ... and he threatens ... He says he is a Red commander ... You'll live with me, he says, in a luxurious home . . . advances every day ... my psyche, he says, is very kind, it's only cats I hate ... He took my ring for a memento ..."

"There, there ... a kind psyche ... From Seville and to Granada," muttered Philip Philippovich. "You must have patience, you are still so young ..."

"Was it really that same gateway?"

"Well, now, take the money when it's offered to you, it's a loan," growled Philip Philippovich.

He solemnly flung the door open, and Bormenthal led Sharikov in at Philip Philippovich's invitation. Sharikov's eyes ran furtively from corner to corner, and the fur on his head stood up like a brush.

"Swine," the young lady said, her tear-stained eyes flashing, her make-up smeared over her cheeks and her streaked, powdered nose.

"Why do you have a scar on your forehead? Kindly tell this lady," Philip Philippovich asked insinuatingly.

Sharikov tried to bluff his way:

"I was wounded fighting Kolchack," he barked.

The young lady got up and went out, weeping loudly.

"Stop it!" Philip Philippovich cried after her. "And wait a moment. The ring, please," he said, turning to Sharikov, who meekly removed the cheap little ring with an emerald stone from his finger.

"All right," he said viciously. "You'll remember it. We'll have a reduction in personnel tomorrow."

"Don't be afraid of him," Bormenthal cried after her. "I will not permit him to do anything." He turned and gave Sharikov a look that made him back away and knock his head against one of the cabinets.

"What is her name?" Bormenthal asked him. "Her name!" he suddenly roared and became terrifying in his fury.

"Vasnetsova," answered Sharikov, his eyes searching for an opportunity to slip away.

Bormenthal took hold of the lapel of Sharikov's jacket and said: "I shall personally make daily inquiries of the purge office to make sure that citizen Vasnetsova has not been fired. And if you . . . if I find out that she was, I will . . . I will shoot you here with my own hands. Look out, Sharikov—I am telling you in plain language!"

Sharikov's eyes were fixed, unblinking, on Bormenthal's nose.

"I can find a revolver or two myself. . . ." mumbled Polygraph, though listlessly. And suddenly, with a quick movement, he freed himself and spurted out through the door.

"Take care!" Bormenthal shouted after him.

The night and the first half of the following day hung heavy like a cloud before a storm. But everyone

was silent. Polygraph Polygraphovich, who had awakened with a pang of nasty premonition, had gone off to
work in the truck in a sullen mood. And a little later,
Professor Preobrazhensky received one of his former
patients at an hour entirely outside his usual schedule.
The visitor, a tall and stout man in a military uniform,
had urgently insisted on seeing the professor, and was
finally given an appointment. Entering the office, he
courteously clicked his heels in greeting the professor.

"Have your pains returned, my friend?" asked the
professor, haggard-faced. "Sit down, please."

"Merci. No, Professor," replied the guest, placing his
peaked helmet on the corner of the table. "I am most
grateful to you . . . Hm . . . I've come in connection
with a different matter, Philip Philippovich . . . my
great regard for you . . . hm . . . to warn you. It's
obvious nonsense. He is simply a scoundrel. . . ." The
patient opened his briefcase and took out a sheet of
paper. "Fortunately, it was reported directly to me. . . ."

Philip Philippovich saddled his nose with pince-nez
over his glasses and began to read. He muttered to
himself for a long time, changing color every second.
". . . and also threatening to kill the house committee
chairman, from which it can be seen that he owns
firearms. And he makes counterrevolutionary speeches,
and even ordered his social servant Zinaida Prokofievna
Bunina to throw Engels into the stove, as an open
Menshevik with his assistant Bormenthal, Ivan Arnoldovich, who secretly lives in his apartment without
registration. Signed, Director of the purge sub-section
P. P. Sharikov—attested to by Chairman of the House
Committee, Shvonder, and Secretary Pestrukhin."

"Will you permit me to keep this?" asked Philip
Philippovich, his face becoming spotty. "But pardon
me, perhaps you need it to pursue the matter further
according to law?"

"I beg your pardon, Professor," the patient said in an extremely offended tone, flaring out his nostrils. "You really take much too contemptuous a view of us. I . . ." and he began to puff himself up like a turkey.

"Oh, forgive me, forgive me, my friend!" muttered Philip Philippovich. "Forgive me, I did not mean to offend you. My dear, don't be angry, I'm at my wits' end with him. . . ."

"I thought so myself," the patient said, entirely mollified, "what a bastard he is, after all! I'd be curious to have a peek at him. Moscow is simply buzzing with all sorts of legends about you. . . ."

Philip Philippovich only spread his hands in despair. The patient looked at him, thinking that the professor had begun to stoop lately, and had turned quite gray.

The crime had ripened, and it fell like a stone, as, indeed, it usually does. Polygraph Polygraphovich returned in the truck with something tugging unpleasantly at his heart. Philip Philippovich's voice invited him into the examination room. The astonished Sharikov entered and glanced wth vague anxiety at the black muzzles staring at him from Bormenthal's face and then at Philip Philippovich. A cloud seemed to move around the assistant, and his left hand, holding a cigarette, was trembling faintly on the shiny arm of the obstetric examination chair.

Philip Philippovich spoke with a calm control that boded no good:

"Take your things immediately—your trousers, your coat, everything you need—and get out of this apartment!"

"How's that?" Sharikov was genuinely surprised.

"Out of this apartment—today," Philip Philippovich repeated monotonously, squinting down at his nails.

Some demon seemed to take possession of Polygraph Polygraphovich. His fate was evidently already lying in wait for him, and the end was just behind his back. He threw himself into the arms of the inevitable and barked out sharply and maliciously:

"What is this, really! You think I won't find justice against you? I have my sixteen *arshin* here, and here I stay."

"Get out of the apartment," Philip Philippovich repeated in a strangled whisper.

Sharikov invited his own death. He raised his left arm toward Philip Philippovich and made an obscene gesture with his scratched fist which reeked intolerably of cats. Then with his right hand, he took a revolver from his pocket and aimed it at the dangerous Bormenthal. Bormenthal's cigarette dropped like a falling star, and a few seconds later Philip Philippovich was rushing back and forth in mortal terror from instrument case to sofa, jumping over broken glass. On the sofa, the director of the purge section lay supine and gurgling, with the surgeon Bormenthal astride his chest and choking him with a small white pillow.

A few minutes later Dr. Bormenthal, his face distorted beyond recognition, went out of the front door and pasted a note near the bell:

"Due to the professor's illness, there will be no visiting hours today. Please do not ring the bell."

With a shiny penknife he cut the bell wire, examined in the mirror his scratched and bloodied face, and then his torn and trembling hands. Then he appeared in the kitchen doorway and told the anxious Zina and Darya Petrovna:

"The professor asks you not to go out anywhere for the present."

"We won't," Zina and Darya Petrovna answered timidly.

"Allow me to lock the back door and take the key with me," said Bormenthal, covering his face with his hand and trying to hide behind the door. "This is only for a short time, and it does not mean that you are not trusted. But somebody may come, and you may be unable to refuse and open. And we must not be disturbed. We are busy."

"All right," replied the women, turning pale. Bormenthal locked the back door, the front door, and the door from the hallway into the foyer and his steps disappeared near the examination room.

Silence shrouded the apartment, crept into every corner. Twilight slithered in—a northern, watchful twilight—in short, murk. True, the neighbors across the yard said afterward that all the lights had been on that night in the examination room, which looked into the yard, and even that they had caught sight of the professor's own cap. . . . This is difficult to verify. It's true, also, that when everything was over, Zina babbled that Ivan Arnoldovich had given her the fright of her life in the office after he and the professor had left the examination room. Ivan Arnoldovich, she said, was squatting on his haunches before the fireplace in the office and feeding a blue copybook into the fire with his own hands—one of those books that were used for keeping records of case histories of the professor's patients! The doctor's face, she said, was altogether green, and all, but all of it . . . covered with scratches. Neither was Philip Philippovich like his usual self that evening. And also . . . However, it may be that the ignorant girl from the Prechistenka apartment was lying . . .

One thing can be vouched for: the apartment that evening was totally and frighteningly quiet.

Exactly ten days after the battle in the examination room, the bell rang sharply in Professor Preobrazhensky's apartment on the Prechistenka.

"Criminal police and investigating officer. Be kind enough to open."

Steps ran and clattered, people came in, and quite a crowd assembled in the brilliantly lit waiting room with new glass in the cases. Two men in militia uniforms, one in a black coat, with a briefcase, a gloating and pale Shvonder, the youth who was a woman, the doorman Fyodor, Zina, Darya Petrovna, and the half-dressed Bormenthal, who was modestly covering his throat without a tie.

The office door opened to let Philip Philippovich out. He emerged in the well-known azure bathrobe, and everybody could see at once that Philip Philippovich had improved in health considerably during the past week. It was the old imperious and energetic Philip Philippovich, who presented himself in his full dignity before his nocturnal guests, and apologized for greeting them in his robe.

"Please don't worry, Professor," the man in civilian clothes replied with great embarrassment. Then he hesitated a moment, and began: "It is most awkward. We have a warrant to search your apartment and," the man threw a sidelong glance at Philip Philippovich, and concluded, "and to make an arrest, depending on the results."

Philip Philippovich narrowed his eyes and asked: "Arrest whom, if I may ask, and on what charges?"

The man scratched his cheek and began to read the paper he had taken from his briefcase:

"Preobrazhensky, Bormenthal, Zinaida Bunina and Darya Ivanova, on the charge of murdering the director of the purge section of the Moscow Communal Property Administration, Polygraph Polygraphovich Sharikov."

Zina's sobs almost drowned the last words. There was a movement in the crowd.

"I don't understand anything," answered Philip Philippovich, raising his shoulders with a royal air. "What Sharikov? Ah, sorry, you mean my dog . . . on whom I operated?"

"If you will pardon me, Professor, not the dog, but when he was already a man. That's the point."

"You mean, he spoke?" asked Philip Philippovich. "But this does not yet mean being a man. However, that is unimportant. Sharik is still alive, and no one has killed him."

"Professor," the black little man said with astonishment, raising his eyebrows, "in that case you will have to produce him. He has been missing ten days, and the indications, if you will excuse me, are quite bad."

"Doctor Bormenthal, be kind enough to present Sharik to the investigating officer," commanded Philip Philippovich, appropriating the warrant. Dr. Bormenthal went out with a crooked smile.

When he returned, he whistled, and a strange dog jumped out after him from the office. He was bald in spots, and his fur was growing back in spots. He came out like a trained circus animal, on his hind legs, then he dropped on all fours and looked around him. Dead silence congealed in the waiting room like jello. The monstrous-looking dog with a purple scar on his forehead rose again to his hind paws and sat down in a chair with a smile.

The second militiaman crossed himself hurriedly and backed away, stepping on both of Zina's feet.

The man in black stuttered without closing his mouth.

"But how . . . allow me . . . He worked at the purge section. . . ."

"I never appointed him there," answered Philip Philippovich. "It was Mr. Shvonder who recomended him, if I am not mistaken."

"I don't unerstand anything," the black one said, totally perplexed, and turned to the first militiaman. "Is that him?"

"It's him," the militiaman answered soundlessly. "It sure is."

"It's him, all right," said Fyodor's voice. "Only he's grown his fur back, the scoundrel."

"But he spoke . . . khe . . . khe . . ."

"He still speaks, but less and less. I would suggest you take advantage of the moment, because he'll soon grow silent altogether."

"But why?" the black man inquired in an undertone.

Philip Philippovich shrugged his shoulders.

"Science has not yet discovered methods of transforming animals into humans. I tried, but unsuccessfully, as you can see. He spoke for a while, and then began to revert to his original state. Atavism."

"No indecent language here!" the dog barked suddenly from his chair and stood up.

The black man blanched suddenly, dropped his briefcase, and began to fall sideways. The militiaman caught him from the side, and Fyodor from behind. Confusion ensued, and in the midst of it three phrases were heard most clearly:

Philip Philippovich's: "Valerian. He has fainted."

Dr. Bormenthal's: "I shall throw Shvonder down the stairs with my own hands if he appears again in Professor Preobrazhensky's apartment."

And Shvonder's: "I demand that these words be entered into the record."

The gray accordions of the radiators hummed. The curtains shut out the dense Prechistenka night with its solitary star. The superior being, the dignified benefactor of dogs, sat in his armchair, and the dog Sharik lay sprawled on the rug near the leather sofa. The March fogs gave the dog headaches in the morning, which gripped him with a ring of pain around the seam on his head. But by evening, the warmth dissipated the pain. And now, too, it was going, going, and the thoughts that flowed through the dog's head were pleasant and warm.

I've been so lucky, so lucky, he thought, dozing off. Just incredibly lucky. I'm set for life in this apartment. I am absolutely convinced that there was something shady in my ancestry. There must have been a Newfoundland. She was a whore, my grandmother, may she rest in the Heavenly Kingdom, the old lady. True, they've slashed up my whole head for some strange reason, but it'll heal before my wedding. It's not worth mentioning.

Glass jars tinkled quietly in the distance. The bitten one was tidying up the instrument cases in the examination room.

And the gray-haired wizard sat, humming:
"Toward the sacred banks of the Nile ..."
The dog witnessed terrible doings. The important
man plunged his hands dressed in slippery gloves
into jars, pulled out brains, a stubborn man, a persistent one, searching for something all the time,
cutting, examining, squinting and singing:
"Toward the sacred banks of the Nile ..."

Moscow
January-March, 1925

Selected Grove Press Paperbacks